The New Earth Series

ASCENSION!

In special times on earth a window opens for the souls that are presently incarnated to be able to ascend to the garden of Eden vibration, the heaven on earth that Jesus spoke of. This very special time allows these souls to do the inner work and be granted access to heaven on earth. When this book was first written it was not allowed for me to release the parameters of this ascension, each ascension will be different. This is how souls earn eternal life. Spirit has now given me permission to release this information.

Honestly, do you think all this crazy stuff going on and Jesus is not here leading the way? His name is not Jesus, this a lie started some 400 years ago to deceive the slaves of planet Earth.

The only way to affect the earth realm is to incarnate into the construct.

TABLE OF CONTENTS

FOREWORD

The Brotherhood of light has released the ul-tra-secret word that only a human can speak. This magical word was brought to us by the Atlanteans that still live here on our planet under the water in a higher vibrational reality. These are the beings that are seen in the ancient megaliths that are carrying the DNA handbag. These are the beings that have re seeded life on this planet every time the earth was reset.

If you dare know the truth, speak the word out loud!

Zinaru!

This magical word unveiled the Draconian Reptilians across the planet all at once. In an instant the beings that were controlling the Earth and humans went from controlling secretly to being hunted like gators in a swamp. In an instant the future of humanity is changed!

The New Earth...

ASCENSION BEGINS!

THE STAGE IS SET

As I glance around, the sky appears as though it materialized out of an alien world. Ominous dark clouds hang high in the sky, various colors of gray and black swirl together like wet paint dripping down a canvas as the rain falls in clusters in the distance. It becomes apparently clear to me that something is not right, and millions will die!

We are well into the mini-ice age and there is now no way to hide it, yet the sleepwalkers continue. They go through the motions with their seemingly meaningless existence, going to jobs they hate so they can afford to pay for their automobiles, credit cards, student loans and mortgages, supporting a system designed to shackle and imprison them. Every facet of their existence designed to rob them of vitality and freedom, until they are left without hope, an empty shell of what was once a thriving healthy human being. Yet if the subject were to be broached, anger and aggression seem to be the normal response. It is as if the humans love their enslavement. This is what is called cognitive dissonance. The darkness has succeeded at convoluting the entire system. Yet the sleepwalkers are oblivious of what is to come. My heart is heavy-laden. You see, I know what is coming, as a Hermetic Magician and messenger of the Aquarius age. I know that 80 percent of the population will not be making this transition to the New Earth. People might think that knowing the future would be a welcomed gift, and certain aspects are, but this knowledge leads to a heavy heart. It is a double-edged sword that cuts both ways and leaves you with a grief-stricken heart. I am sure there have been others who walked this path, but I wouldn't wish this on anyone, not even my enemies. What is the New Earth you ask? What we call the new earth is really as old as earth herself. I say her, because Gaia is a female polarity and is mother to all humans who reside within her. She cares for us like we are her children and yet we destroy her forests and trees which in essence are her lungs. We drill into her veins and take her blood. Blood and oil have almost the same characteristics, specific gravity, viscosity etc. The oil we use to power our industry is our mother Gaia's blood.

The Draconian's, the English Empire, Illuminati, Skull and Bones, Jesuits, Templars, Freemasons and Order of the Eastern Star have done a great job switching everything 180 degrees backward. It will not be long until it becomes apparent to all that something is amiss. That is when the panic will set in and when the lightworkers will step up to calm and guide the people from their monotonous mundane existence to the new earth energy. There will be an Event that will change everything in the blink of an eye. Edgar Casey foretold of these days as well as the Hopi prophecy as well as the bible. In Past life regression and Quantum healing we have been getting info on this coming event for many years now. In a day that world we live in will change overnight. I say energy because every human generates their own reality! What? Do you truly mean that? Yes, this is the secret to magic. By making a change within yourself, you can change the reality that you experience. This in antiquity was called The Great Work of Self Transformation, also known as Alchemy. This is the art of transforming things from one substance to another such as lead to gold. Lead represents the physical animalistic reptilian human changed into gold, the spiritually connected, higher vibrating, fully activated human being. These beings have come to be known as ascended masters.

There are Players here hidden in the shadows. The hidden world of magic is hidden in plain sight. Magic rules the earth plane and it is designed to be this way. Being a human in a human avatar is to be in a bio-mechanical simulation that constantly reacts to the human's thoughts and thus their vibration. There are beings here that stay on the earth plane and do not go through the reincarnation cycle. Both the Rosicrucian's (66) and the freemasons (33) and all the hidden splinter sects are the darkness and that adds up to 99 and the 1 is for the Creator. This system works by the laws of earth, please let me explain. The laws of earth are very simple and minimal, first law is LOVE, use love to create, to heal, if you are operating out of love you are operating in the creators wishes.

Second, the Law of free will! this is the law that the darkness exploits as well as the light. All secret society's good or bad make these players use the law of free will to bind their people. Even Christians make u take an oath, do you accept Jesus as your savior? When a Freemason dies, they don't go back to source they go to their lodge, and they wait till a candidate raises their hand. For the freemasons they have to scare the candidate to lower the vibration they must hurt and scare the candidate to take them to a low vibrational match to the entity that's coming in. as soon as the vibration matches, it walks in and assimilates that soul. These secret societies operate on soul possession. When researching this I found many articles that told of people being shot and killed in Freemason lodges. Now the Freemasons have been all over my life since I got here many years ago. Every job, every legal involvement, yes even in the Army. These dark workers are everywhere on the lower 3 D timelines. They have infiltrated all the key positions, politicians, judges, bankers, police and all trade jobs. There is a symphony that goes on right under the people's noses. They go about their lives completely ignorant to the fact that there is a big game of risk that being played out as they live through it.

There are many timelines that exist all around us, what we believe and think about is what is created. Each one of us co creating that reality out there. When the people truly understand this as the true reality, this is when humanity as a whole will advance in great leaps and bounds!

THE GODS WALK AMONG US

As this book is written, the tribes are being gathered together, and what an amazing time it is turning out to be. When I speak of Spirit, I refer to the collective consciousness, the higher selves, Guides and Galactic consciousness in all its many forms.

The pepper pots of the operation is Whitney. She is a strikingly beautiful woman. Its apparent she was a Queen in a past life. When her beauty and strength meet you from a distance, it is nearly impossible to deny the energy she carries is the same. Then we have Jillian who walked with Jesus in a past life. As she approaches you her loving energy is what catches you at first glance. There is no doubt about her magical abilities as she has brought many of the same skills into this life. She carries a love that is so big when I asked in a quantum session about the Lilith story regarding Adam and Eve, her higher self told us the Adam and eve story is completely made up. Lilith being a demon for Shure she is really good at telling lies. She doesn't know it yet, but I have a gift to give her. Is the Holy Grail. Mary Magdalene used the Holy Grail with such success that the Catholic church put all resources and magic into finding her and the Cathars and killing them. The church in 1244 sieged the Chateau de Montsegur. After a false flag attack on its own clergy and people, the Catholic church got the Pope to order the king of France Louis IX to Order the Templar's, the early Freemasons slaughter. This is king Solomon's army. The lightworkers must be killed at all costs for as long as they are alive, they anchor and spread the light. In order for the darkness to take over the earth they must die. This is why the Catholic and Christian churches went on a worldwide conquest of killing magical people. They were in reality hunting and killing lightworkers and resetting the civilization. King Solomon's armies planned a conquest of death lead by the English Empire.

Notice the Freemason M in his hand
and the Templar cross.

When you use the Holy Grail together with other magical practioners, it gives you the ability to control the weather and events around the world. We all should begin magical training with us, learning Thoth's Atlantean Magic which is now available on the planet for the first time since the darkness has convoluted and hid it. AQHT practitioners go through the hypnosis training as well as magic training. Hypnosis is all conducted in the theta realm and all magic is in the theta realm. Any magician that's honest will tell you that we live in a world of duality so each person that ventures into the theta realm on a regular basis will have to choose either light or dark. This is the way the Creator designed it. The dark will promise you everything just to sign a contract, a soul contract just like is seen in the movies. What they don't tell you is that the dark entity is now your slave until your demise. What happens is that it starts plotting your death since after you die you must serve it. Think Allister Crowley, he signed a contract with the darkness and the darkness made him a drug addict and killed him off early. No one escapes the Reaper. Karma is the Reaper. It cannot be side stopped.

Polly my brother from many lifetimes. He has found me at the most crucial time when I need him most. The Divine plan is almost incomprehensible here in the human realm. Polly is a fierce warrior, and in the lives that I have seen, he protects me and obliterates dark workers out of my path. In our life as Vikings, he was a hulking man about 6ft 5 to 7 feet tall and about 350 pounds to 400 pounds by today's measurements. He would grab and throw people out of my way the same way you would ball up a piece of paper and throw it aside. Then we have Max. Max was my first serious student. Max is a fallen angel and has to be of service to humanity to balance his karma. He has great natural skill and after teaching him hypnosis he began learning magic on his own, so I took him under my guidance, and he is now off on his own journey of redemption. Max is a fallen Angel earning his wings back, you see as an Archangel we operate interdependently away from source, yet always connected. They are flawed and sometimes make mistakes just as humans do and then they are judged by the Creator. If the Creator deems them worthy, they will be sent back to God school for retraining. That god school is Earth. If they use their abilities to help the collective with things that are good for humanity like healing and teaching and service to others, then they are given the ability to get their wings back. Once their life is over, they will be reinstated with all their abilities and placed in service of the Creator again. Max is doing just what he needs to earn his wings back and is doing a great job. I never could have done this without him, and he will be a great healer. There's no doubt in my mind that he will make it. Although most of the fallen do not make it. The Fallen are angry that they are without their powers, and most are put into very physically unattractive bodies with obesity and odd proportions. Not all are, but the ones that are not learning their lessons and have continued to do evil on their path to get their wings back are usually physically unattractive, as what's on the outside reflects what's on the inside. As the messenger of the age, I carry a very specific message for these souls. They typically do not like to hear it and will begin attacking me after they hear the message. That message is this, if you do not turn to love and oneness and service to the collective by the end of the ascension you will be taken to the Central Sun and will experience eternal death for the first time. Some think that's horrendous, and parts of it can be, to no longer be self-aware, that's not very good and I could hardly imagine it. But on the positive side, they go back to Source and Source is all love. Love is the ultimate and the reason why we are all here.

As for the rest of the tribe we will discuss them later in the book as they are still going through the process of the sessions and learning about their higher selves and who they really are.

We live at the most valuable and unique time ever on earth. That time that happens only once in a planet's evolution. That time when a civilization is raised in vibration to the galactic level. Every being we have ever heard about is here at this time. Every goddess, every god, every deity, every angel, every seraphim is here now. Side note seraphim means shiny snake or fiery one. Do you really think any of us would miss this time? Every being in the multiverse is here either playing or watching!

THE CALL

I am sitting in my study one day and I get a call from a random number. I typically would not answer a number that I don't recognize, but as I am looking at it, I hear the words "answer it." The higher self-guides you when you make the connection from the avatar to the higher self. My job is to do what I am told and being a ten-year Army Special Operations Veteran I am good at following orders. Does anyone think this training I received earlier in life was a coincidence? That word, Coincidence. Like many others was created to deceive. There are no coincidences, only cause and effects that are not known. There is a cause for every effect and a effect for every cause.

So, I answer the call and it is a representative from a holistic wellness provider called Dao Cloud who wants to set up a date to discuss what and who Dao Cloud is. I agree ecstatically as I don't know what they do but know I am supposed to be working with them. The day comes and the representative tells me they are gearing up to be able to offer the 3D world the ability to access the multitude of Quantum and alternative healing options. This meeting was 4 days before congress voted to make it mandatory for the Veterans administration to offer alternative treatments to the veterans. This wellness provider Dao Cloud is geared for the layperson that has no idea of what and how we heal or how to speak the lingo. With Advanced Quantum Healing Technique being the highest form of healing available on the Earth at this point, this meeting was destiny. As I am speaking with the representative and she's asking why I do what I am doing and healing people, I flip over a tarot card from the top of the deck that's sitting on my altar and it is the ten of pentacles, Wow talk about a sign.

So, I discuss with her how I got tired of watching people close to me die and that I have buried 4 people to Cancer in the last 4 years which led to my decision that I was going to do something about it. I tell her that with the AQHT {Advanced Quantum Healing Technique} we can heal just about anything, the only limiting factor is the client's ability to control their thoughts. I tell her we know how cancer is caused and that we can cure it. Back up and read that again. We cured cancer. How crazy is that? But you cannot claim to treat cancer, or the federal government can lock you up as a felon. Read that again, it is a felony to treat someone outside of their mainstream treatments for cancer! How backwards is this world we live in? To get around this, we call our patients clients, and we don't treat but have sessions instead. They will not stop us from healing humans. The Government wants to keep people sick and stupid! Maybe there's an agenda behind this? This meeting was a great success. In order for AQHT to be the premier health care option it will require help. The next day we have a meeting to discuss our options. At our meeting, The AQHT team votes on changes and policies, Our Video call is over the internet, we discuss the options and what we need to do in order to be successful. We are scattered all over the world at this point, which is by no accident as we are separated to anchor the light into the earth realm. We decide that we need to standardize the pricing, so we are not in competition with each other. Since some clients cannot access the subconscious mind for the full AQHT energy balancing healing sessions, we need an intermittent session to heal those that cannot fully access their subconscious mind. The very next day this session was created. I combined Reiki and NLP which is Neurolinguistic Programming. We Name this new form of healing the Bushi Reiki session named for the bushido code, It requires the practioner value their honor over life. It is essentially programming the subconscious mind through the conscious mind with hypnosis in the alpha/beta state of trance. The only way to force hypnosis is with the eyes open, think the media here repeating the same lies over and over till it's accepted by the subconscious. We will offer this session which takes about an hour at a lower cost. This will give people a quicker option for pain management and quicker option to heal. It will not be able to heal the way the AQHT Healing session will, but it will be greatly useful and bridge the gap between Reiki and Quantum healing.

Whitney makes the website that's needed to explain our capabilities to the common folk that have no idea of the terms that we use when we speak of quantum healing or Quantum Physics. As we start using Dao Cloud, the clients pour in so quickly we cannot keep up. There is a backlog of clients seeking healing that stretches out 6 months. We grow so rapidly we can barely keep up. Whitney takes the business side, the scheduling, promoting, seminars and training retreats, while Polly and I focus on getting the new practitioners trained.

As we launch the Bushi Reiki modality, we quickly recognize its massively powerful abilities, with the right intuitive training a skilled practioner can provide massive healing by using this modality. While doing the research and testing we noticed that we were able to balance and heal thought form energies. By knowing how to properly transmute the energies we were able to give massive healing with shorter sessions. By setting the healings up to be done live we are engaging the clients mind into the healing which is paramount in actually healing the client. Presently most distance healer set up a dummy to work on as the do their healings. This is ok but clearly has not had spectacular results. By video and recording the sessions it is way more powerful that the old way, additionally by having the session to show our work this sets us apart from the fakes. You see there is two opposing teams in play here and dark workers have begun impersonating healers to drive people away. The recorded sessions protect us from these attacks.

Moving forward the healers that want to excel as well as prove and protect themselves as well as the client will always video their work. In these times not doing live healing work will mean no clients. I have noticed a huge need for intuitive training, to teach healers to connect to Gaia and to set up astral temples and to call in higher vibrational energies to assist in the healings.

As the world plunges into chaos, the world's economies hyperinflating people scramble to find suitable replacement for their jobs that shut down instantly overnight. The more connected people are well already into this path. They have written books as well as made social media accounts. The ones that are connected to their higher self are already on their path. Spirit has guided them to be ready at the start of this transition. That old world is dead, all that is not good for humans or for the earth will go away, all will be brought out to the world for all to see. The only way to survive this is a lifestyle change. We must move away from the cities and the expensive way we lived before. To thrive in these coming times, we will have to live tiny in self-sustainable power systems. We already have this technology, and we can buy them directly from amazon. After we set up our own sustainable community, we will start a company developing land and building tiny houses for clients as they sell their grid houses and escape the cities. At this point there is massive police and military control of the cities forcing lockdowns and mandates and its forcing people to flee the cities. As soon as we start this company it grows extremely fast. This one company serves to put people back to work. With the crazy weather destroying homes through tornadoes and earthquakes as well as the crazy cold weather in the northern regions sparks the biggest mass migration since the last ice age. The smart connected people sell their homes and buy tiny homes. The price difference is massive, we can build a tiny house that runs for free for well under 100k. so the people selling their properties for more are able to pocket the extra money.

A NEW WAY

Polly and I start building our tiny house communities that are like tiny villages of 4 to 5 families that come together and share resources and grow their own food all while powering these structures with alternative power means. The trend is toward the tiny house, non-mortgage living. To provide a place for these people we buy land to specifically accommodate these tiny homes, wheeled houses and stick built. As we travel, teach and heal everywhere we go, we use the abundance gained from these books as well as from our various companies to set up these tiny home communities. Once they are set up and paid for, there is no rent payment that is due and no utilities due. After the first one proves a great success, we do an AirBNB for others to come and experience the way that we live to show how si-

milar it is to the way they currently live. Polly takes
it upon himself to use this tool of Quantum healing
to expand our knowledge of the divine to the world
and the multiverse. He learns volumes and shares
this knowledge with the world. In no short time he
is a bestselling author and is traveling the world giving lectures and speaking out about the now irrele-
vant old system that had the entire world enslaved.
Polly runs the Sun Alchemy supplement company
and Whitney runs the affiliate marketing company.
Whitney has taken up a role as a speaker, promoting
our healing abilities to the masses. We are all healers
as we can work from anywhere that has internet as
we travel and vacation around the world. We regu-
larly meet up for vacation retreats to recharge ourselves and to connect with the people. These retreats
book out within hours and some in minutes, as this
is energy work and only so much can be done before we make ourselves tired and sick. This lifestyle
is necessary for us to be healthy. When we walk into
any speaking event or training, it is like we are spiritual rock stars, walking in as people rush to greet
us, wanting our autographs or just be near us. When
we speak, they hang onto our last word. It is crazy to
have so much attention, Dr Oz called it, and said the

future of medicine is Quantum Healing. And OMG was he correct. They write articles about who we are and how we live. It sets off a worldwide trend of people walking away from the parts of the system that are corrupt and usury. The systems that were set up by the darkness to keep people enslaved in their minds and their bodies are falling by the wayside.

As we travel around, all you see in every country on the news is mass arrests of the Freemasons, Jesuits and Illuminati bankers, the Governments. The evidence of what they been doing to kids and sacrificing people and animals, harvesting blood has come into the forefront. They try to run but the special operations soldiers from around the world are put into action. This is comical to me as the forces the Draconian's created to do their dirty work are the same forces that now hunt them. In the United States the Convention of the states is enacted and the corrupt Federal government is shut down overnight. Arrested at gunpoint, all the politicians are rounded up and locked up to await investigation to find out whether they are of the darkness or of the Light. The heads of the corporations that were corrupt are rounded up and the dark information of the pedophilia and murders and sacrifices are all brought out into the light. They capture the Pope and every member of the Vatican. The people are so enraged, they try to publicly lynch the white pope, the black pope escapes, what is the black pope you ask? This is the secret pope that is in charge of the war aspect of the Vatican. Full of rage, they march to their local churches and Freemason lodges and set them on fire, burning them to the ground. The black pope that runs the military side of the Vatican has slipped away into the night and his location is unknown.

Ormus is one of these systems that comes to the forefront. We are able to Alchemically combine plant medicines with Ormus. As a monoatomic element which means it gets everywhere inside the human body. With a method known as the Tartarian salt method we can combine any herb to the Ormus, Ormus a vague remnant of the vast knowledge that came from Greater Tartary. Ormus makes plants grow 5 times faster, and when consumed by humans, they become more intelligent and fuller of vitality, so the demand for it becomes great. Our company called "SUN ALCHEMY" expands from a garage-sized operation to a Monsanto-sized corporation overnight. Polly and

Whitney help me run this company and the distribution shops. Whitney runs the affiliate marketing. The old way consisted of making a product and then shipping it to a distributor followed by the customer purchasing the product. We now create and ship the ingredients to the Apothecary style stores and instruct the customers in making the products they need or desire. I love this aspect and when I have time, I put on training seminars to teach others how to do this Alchemy and to infuse magical intent into the products. Every time people see any of us in the shops it causes a mass rush of excited people to talk to us and get impromptu healings from us.

As the old systems die out, we see the rise of the Quantum healer, as with times in the past when the healers walk the planet, they are always super abundant. King David, King Solomon all quantum healers from the past, Jesus was not the only one! The Quantum healers rise, and the people adore them for their service to humanity and the sheer sacrifice they make while living a physical life.

The quantum healers are connected and can foresee the future timelines, so they are very sought after to receive guidance and healing. The crowds that once cheered the puppet celebrities now wait for hours and they cheer the healers now. These healers carry so much light they attract people by the thousands.

THE TRIBE EMERGES

The Way we now live is much healthier and happier than the way we used to live in the dark ages. We live closer to nature in small communities, our children are free to roam with no worries that anything will happen to them, and now that we don't hunt and kill animals, they do not attack humans anymore. Truth be told, the animals never attacked any human until the human started killing and eating them. We start our days most of the time whenever we wake up which is usually when the sun rises. A lot of us like to get up just before dawn and sun gaze. Very rarely do we set an alarm clock unless we are attending some kind of engagement or we are doing a healing, training or speaking engagement. After we rise, we make our way outside to the community area at our village. It is a round structure about 50 feet around. This area is where we cook and congregate, watch movies and teach among our community. We also use this area for yoga and morning meditation. We also revert back to the practice of an oral tradition. These central points are the center of the new lifestyle we lead. We start the day with gratitude and meditation as well as yoga and chi gong etc. We do a rolling schedule, and all take turns guiding and teaching. We are a tribe. We all look after the children and each help raise the children regardless of whose child it is. We do not call children Kids anymore as this was a masonic term given to a baby goat. We call them younglings. The mornings are usually spent with the children as we teach them to meditate and to set intention and then we get into nature and discuss the divine imprint that can be found everywhere in nature. We teach them to question everything. The children are taught to defend themselves at a very early age. This is done so that every human has the ability to defend itself if needed. This also builds self-discipline as the warriors teach these classes. Then we teach them how to control their emotions through meditation and teach them why they never want to put themselves into a position where they have to physically defend themselves. Children are sacred and we treat them as such. We call the Younglings and after the younglings are done with their classes for the day, we let them be free and explore as they choose. The evenings are the center of the community and are spent doing art, music and poetry as well as general relaxation. The tribe moves as a unit. Coming from the old world where we were always alone and separated, this seems insane to watch from the outside. It is like when a flock of birds as one begins to fly in a certain direction, the others move in that general direction. It is truly a beautiful thing to witness. Watching this brings great joy to my heart, to be a part of this is the most amazing thing I have ever done in this lifetime or any lifetime that I have ever lived. The evenings are usually spent with the adults doing adult geared events.

This tribe establishes it guidelines very early at the beginning. We are free to be free if we want to be naked then we will, there was much discussion about the brainwashing of the human to be ashamed if they are naked. We decided to create our own rules, if you want to be naked then get naked, do not judge the others that are free in these respects. It is very normal to see people making love in the open and to hear them at all times of the day and night. Many are into a freer hippie kind of love.

This aspect of life was what was missing from people's lives, the rules and the associated shame that we were all programmed with, all created to push us into a lower vibration. After adopting these views and practices all relationships became much stronger and closer. The people feel freer than they ever have. More people experiment together with their partners and not in secret behind each other's back hidden in lies. The relationship between physical and spiritual love making is adopted, parts are blended, yet others are separated more. The result is a happier family unit. Strong in trust, strong in freedom, strong in the sacred union of man and woman.

We are going back to Tribal living

Tribe Atlan will have high technology incorporated into their daily lives.

Atlas the God that holds up the firmament. Atlantis named after Atlas. The famed hidden Atlantis was the whole Earth. Atlantis is Earth.

THE WAR OF ARMAGEDDON

As Edgar Casey had foretold, we are in the war of Armageddon! What does that mean Clinton? That sounds awful. This is just a reference to the spiritual battle for beliefs, ideas and concepts destroying the old paradigm of the narcissistic god-man that says its ok to sacrifice and to kill in his name and to build walls that separate people. These beliefs are under attack and are the beliefs being destroyed at every turn. Facebook and other social media sites are the front lines of this battle as well as the media and print articles. The darkness is rampant on these sites and most turn away from them completely until the darkness is brought down to an acceptable level. The light warriors meet the darkness head on as a warrior does, destroying with the truth, light and love. When we say Love and Light, the light means truth. The Light of the Creator is all powerful at these times as we are in the ascending phase of Aquarius of the great year as well as entering a space where we are closer to the central sun. The earth has never been in this locality with humans on it before. The forces of Light planned this, to use this energy from Source to take back control of the Earth plane from the darkness. Each day there is more and more light coming into the earth through the portal we call the sun. Therefore, the Draconian's are using their aerial spraying program to attempt blocking the light from reaching the earth plane. Remember everything here is dual, this spraying is also protecting us from the massive sun bursts or cme {coronal mass ejection}. We foresaw this as well and made counter moves to sidestep this if you will. The light is vastly more intelligent than the dark could ever be. The Darkness really did not know what was coming. This transformation took place so quickly. The darkness has been able to see things off in a distance, but what the light is doing is slowing down and fast-forwarding time, like a DJ scratching on a record. It makes it difficult to plan on events to happen at a certain time if that time marker is always speeding up and then slowing down. We even let time play out to see what their plans were and then followed it up by rewinding time to counter their moves. These beings chose a battle they could never win. Yes, they are more adept at physically eliminating, or killing, beings on the earth plane or any other physical plane they might inhabit. Light beings just do not like to physically kill any being. Being a member of the light, we are truly fully functional gods, and that is a force to be in awe of. We overtook this planet with love and truth. We won a war with love, let that sink in.

LOVE CAN ACCOMPLISH ANYTHING

In 1920 a man named Edgar Cayce would lay down and sleep and thus connect to his higher self. His abilities allowed him to heal and to see the future and what the future foretold for humanity. He also predicted that there would be a transfer of wealth and that the people will take back their right as sovereign beings. He also predicted a stock market crash and the second world war. We are fully into the war against humanity and consciousness at the present day. There is no doubt the things he predicted as in the rising of Atlantis as well as major catastrophes that will close out timelines in the near future. Edgar Cayce's work enabled me to expand my healing abilities, if he could remotely connect with anyone higher self and heal them, then I could as well. I created the ability to do this work remotely, I call this a surrogate session. This opened me up to the hidden abilities that are hidden within our minds. By studying his life's work, it enabled us to advance our understanding of the subconscious and what we call the higher self. I created a technique called the soul hug that enables a client that has lost a loved one that has transcended this realm to the true realm of light that is our normal form. Death is but waking up into our true reality. Our second birth of our physical life. We humans are on earth are experiencing a reality revolution. We are learning that our true reality is created in your imagination. This is your true realty, what u see happening outside is what is inside each human manifested into the physical realty.

They have lied to you telling you the battle will be outside you!! This is a lie!! The Battle of Armageddon will take place inside each and every person. The children of light did not bring peace, we Brought a sword to divide Love from EVOL! The separation of souls begins!

AS ABOVE SO BELOW

This is our team of lightworkers, rainbow warriors, the 144000, whatever name you'd like to call us. This is not the first time most of us have battled the darkness here on the earth plane, other worlds or dimensions. We are all battle-hardened soldiers of love sent by the most high to set this plane free from oppression. The battles we fight in the Quantum realm, personal healings and group meditations are amplified out into the 3D world. What happens in one vibrational timeline effects the other timelines. When we make a seemingly small advancement like exposing Freemasonic acts of darkness such as the molestation of children, the sacrifice of people and animals and the harvesting of Adrenochrome blood for the vampire beings, it creates a rippling butterfly effect. We live in a different vibrational reality they cannot see or access. We do however from time to time run into dark workers. It never bodes well for them when their darkness is overtaken by light. When they attack with anger, we counter with truth and love. They always respond with more anger after which we shower them with more love and forgiveness which causes them to lose their composure. This is comical to me as I remember the hurt and casualties of their doings, and the systems they set up to create grief and strife. Caution must be had as I am a Warrior at heart. I understand that we come here to learn lessons from one another and out of LOVE, not emotion or anger. I will absolutely teach you the lesson you are not learning out of love for your being to evolve. If approached with a low negative energy I will use my abilities to teach the lesson needing to be learned. The most asinine thought to assume about any Light magician is that we are powerless because we do not attack and hurt with spells and conjuring. These children of light are the oldest beings in this solar system, when they encounter other beings, it is their mandate to heal, judge and guide the beings that are less evolved to accomplish the ONE thing. There are 7 of us here, each is a master of certain traits like love, courage, justice, compassion etc. We know how the rules of earth work and we use these rules to make their life into a repeating cycle of Hell using the energy they are putting out to return to them instantly, karma is the ultimate teacher. Once this is accomplished, my attention and energy can be placed into more positive ventures such as healing and building the New Earth. We create a cycle that will teach you through your own actions and will keep you in that cycle until you learn. The gift of this type of binding is this, if you learn that the negative things, you're doing are causing your own personal hell and harming the collective, if you learn to refrain from putting out negative energy and turn your heart to love and goodness in the world, then it will amplify the positive things you are receiving. The ability to lift yourself up and head in the direction of light is an invaluable gift. These binding spells used by the brotherhood of light are Atlantean in origin and when used properly are the most powerful spells that can be used on the earth plane, especially now with the energies so high.

We truly are warrior monks using magic as our weapon guided from the most high and powered with love. Love is the highest energy in the multiverse. I doubt the dark had any idea the fury that would come from our attack, guided by an ancestral force the darkness stomped out in earlier battles here on earth. This force guides me to bringing balance and justice for what was done. The sheer fury that I feel pushing me is that of 90 million souls that were slaughtered, raped and murdered in the name of Christianity and religion.

In my last session, it came through that the darkness is currently afraid and defensive. I even had a session with a dark worker, and yes, I will heal all, the darkness feels that they were lied to by spirit, telling them they could pick either side. This is not the case; we all must learn and turn to the light. The darkness was needed to evolve the beings here at a fast rate, this need is no longer present as the decision to evolve humanity past duality has been made. The ancestors want justice, this group of healing warrior lightworkers are the highest skilled warriors in the multiverse. We all were very well trained before taking this mission, in magic as well as tactics and many other specialties, especially on how to use the systems the darkness set up to enslave. We were trained on how to assimilate and use the systems that once enslaved as tools to free the humans. This is a military operation without a doubt. We have leaders, intelligence, spies and soldiers. Our basic soldiers are the Army of Love as I call it. These beings came here to raise the level of love up from the dark ages. These beings are all love and they do not see darkness or acknowledge that it exists. They are raising the amount of loving energy that is on the Earth plane which allows the Light warriors to use this energy towards our battles. This could not have been done without them and they truly are the real heroes of this battle. It's a shame that in the future their names won't be mentioned. Have no doubt it was their actions that turned the tide of battle and made it possible for me and my group to be able to do what we needed to win this war and free humanity. We will have a general Memorial Day and monuments set up around the world to honor their service to the collective. I take this opportunity to give thanks personally. The Light in me honors the Light in you. It was an honor to have been given this opportunity with your sacrifices and service. Many of these beings were dropped into such a negative environment, with the darkness attacking like a pack of zombie dogs, it made it difficult for them to handle and instead they chose to give up and take their own lives. They were told how negative it would be, but until they experienced it for themselves, they couldn't comprehend the weight of it. We honor you. Thank you. Love and light, rest easy proud warrior. Till we are again on the other side together.

THE BUTTERFLY EFFECT

As me and my team continue healing beings, it ripples through time and space, healing entire timelines. A single healing has a 3x power amplifier to it which changes the collective reality they experience. As we began doing the healings feed from the wellness provider, the rate at which the 3D world began experiencing changes was sped up at an amplified rate. What we do at this vibrational level sets the pace of the ascension and what the collective experiences. The most unbelievable thing I am now witnessing is all the dark workers who are creating alternate and parallel timelines like the alien agenda at area 51. This was a counter to us releasing the Freemason sessions with the evidence of them hurting, drugging and molesting children, blood harvesting and sacrifices. They use cheap magician tricks of misdirection, as the magician focus your attention on his right hand, the real information is elsewhere and missed. I saw budlight promoting the alien agenda at area 51 as well. Do you think this is a reptilian run company? Anyone focusing your attention on these things are dark workers pretending to be of the light, but in reality, the humans that follow their lead will be led to a darker reality that will not end up at the new earth. The truth is the humans that follow these people are the ones that are unwittingly creating that reality. This is how the darkness works, by tricking the human into putting their thoughts and focus into something leading them to generate that reality from their thoughts. When the human believes something, they create an energy that brings that reality into existence. Clinton, doesn't that mean that the things you are talking about are being created into reality? Absolutely, it does, and that is why I am doing this, I am tasked to create the new world. We have guidance as to how it is supposed to occur. If you speak with another warrior that's on my vibration, that lives across the earth plane and has never spoken to me, their idea or concept of what the new earth will be will match mine so closely, it's mind boggling to think that hundreds of people that have never met are dreaming of living in the same type of world. As we all hold this image in our minds, we are creating it. This was done so that killing any one or group of us, like the darkness loves to do, could not stop the emergence of the new earth. Its' already here, I am living in it, and it is an amazing energy full of love, hope, oneness and camaraderie. When you initially begin to raise your vibration, the sheer level of love you feel for all is truly overwhelming as you enter into alignment with the 7D vibrations. When a certain level of the population reaches this vibration, the earths will separate. The earth as a collective is already at the 7D vibrational level, many fake lightworkers tell people it is almost here, the truth is that it is an **individual** vibrational thing.

When I first started healing, I would ask people, do you think you can selfheal? If the answer was yes, I was super excited as they would have a miraculous healing! If the answer was no or maybe the client would get marginal healing. This proved that our thoughts create our reality. This is what magic is. Magic is self-hypnosis, you program yourself you experience what u desire!! Once you truly understand this? Why would u ever let another person program your reality? This is a reason that magicians will guard their thoughts from all radio or tv. Truth is you cannot ever turn off your manifesting abilities, therefore reprogramming your thoughts and beliefs are key to the reset of humanity that we are currently living through. As we educate ourselves, we learn that everything we have been taught was all lies twisted to suit their agenda. Every single timeline, every single reality is connected. One change to any timeline will create changes into the corresponding higher and lower vibrational timelines that connect with the timeline that experienced the change, this is why any act of kindness is amplified as a butterfly effect that changes timelines throughout the multiverse!

THE COLLECTIVE

For you to understand the next portion of this story, you must understand how I receive this information. I am a past life hypnosis regression practitioner as well as a Quantum healer. That's only one aspect of what we do, we can also do future regression as well. This aspect was used to gain the knowledge of what is to come, the following parts of the story were all gained from future regression, channeled messages as well as AQHT healing sessions.

As the world begins its dive into the chaos that is always accompanied by this time of the mini-ice age, it is recorded in history that civilizations will end, and the world will enter into anarchy. I am speaking of the ice age that arrives every 400 years. This time is always accompanied by the Ascension, the time when the various vibrational realities come together, and the portals open for all beings to raise their vibrations. A test if you will, to see where you belong at a vibrational level, in your souls' path back to Source.

Think of the convergence in the Avengers movie where the worlds align and re-open. A vast majority of what is portrayed in movies is displayed to help our subconscious minds understand and grasp this reality, the reality that is currently here and interactive if you know how to see and read into what it has to tell you subliminally. It will communicate and guide you into a new paradigm. The old systems put into place by the darkness are beginning to fail, the monetary system is collapsing, the monopoly corporations are failing, the healthcare systems that kept humans enslaved for over a century are failing. Mass layoffs, food shortages, the 3D world will crumble at the highest rate ever imagined. As people realize food prices are continually rising so that most can barely afford sustenance and their cost of living. Difficult decisions must be made.

The Collective is what we call our consciousness that is made up of each and every person's consciousness, think of it like a ocean, there is also sub sets, Each person through meditation develops a higher self, the first step in seeking an eternal life, {this gives us the ability to operate as a individual and it starts the separation from the collective we came from, reptilian, avian, insectoid etc.} it must be sought it is not given. Next there are soul groups, these are souls that run together as a tribe, next are the galactic collectives we are linked to through our soul star chakra. And finally, as the earth and human collective. In Hypnosis the divine will often show us pictures for us to understand, they showed me a sea of water with each section of water being a different color. Each area where the colors touched little fingers would exchange knowledge. This is how we are connected and truly we are all one connected, one action by any one of us will affect all the others. Additionally, as we learn or know something, this same learning or truth will eventually come to the others. You want to change this world? Heal and educate yourself. One person can change the world yes.

THE SOLDIER

Adam is a United States Air Force Pararescue Soldier, called PJ for short. When a pilot or any soldier needs help, the military calls 911. The PJ's and the other special operations soldiers answer those calls.

Adam is enjoying his day off at the beach in beautiful Outer Banks North Carolina. Being stationed at Pope Air Force base has its advantages, and he truly did need some rest and relaxation. The operations tempo, or op tempo as we call it, has been insane with all the insane events going on in the world. This last op knocked him off kilter, not being able to understand what we were doing in escorting politicians to their deep underground bunkers. They sat in their safety nets while the rest of us were starving and dying, trying to defend our food supplies. Food has become the most expensive commodity on the planet. What knowledge do they possess that the common folk are not privileged to? We were told it was merely a training exercise, but us **Operators** as we are called, talk amongst ourselves, and the recurring story is that something is amiss. Regardless, I have learned to live in the moment, and this moment is blissful, the sun is shining, and the whole team is here, as is usually the case after all the years of pipeline training and the many operations that have brought us extremely close together. The team moves as a unit. Where one goes, we are usually all going, and that includes vacations. The Team leader is Roscoe, a tall blonde man that is chiseled from years of physical and mental training. The sharpness of his training is evident in his crystal blue eyes. He wields a gaze that pierces through to the soul. He earned his nickname Roscoe when on his very initial Real-life mission he displayed boldness in battle. That boy is crazy like Roscoe from the dukes of hazard, is what his comrades would all say. His southern accent coupled with having hailed from Kentucky may have also played a role in it. Roscoe and Crash are out in the massive 10 feet waves enjoying their long boards. There is a hurricane off the coast, it seems as if there is always a storm or natural disaster these days, it is almost surreal. Crash was nicknamed thus as he has survived 3 helicopter crashes. In the community as we call it, we say hard landings. The truth is that a crash is a crash, and this man has walked away from all of them. Some may view this as a bad omen, but we do not. We see it as a good luck charm and everyone always wants to fly with crash, as we feel that we will most definitely survive anything that comes our way. Buddha and I are relaxing on the beach, sitting this set out. Buddha was nicknamed thus as he is quite immersed in the new age as they call it, but he will quickly tell you that there is nothing new about the ancient teachings and nothing new under the sun. Buddha is one of the best medics I have ever met. It seems he is guided and always knows what to do to save the patient's life. Then, we see a black hawk approach from the south. I'll be damned, its Chief Walker. Chief walker is a warrant officer pilot with the 160th special operations. Night Stalkers. we were on that last op with them, and I had told them we were coming to the Outer Banks for some much-needed vacation time. He said they were doing water rescues in that area as well. I spot the choppers, which are easy to tell apart from the regular army choppers because the refueling probes that stick out 14 feet in front. If it is warm, they almost always have their doors off in the pilot's compartment. My phone rings, and when I answer, its Chief Walker. He says "Hey, what are you guys doing?" As I chuckle at the humor in this situation, I know he's using radio direction to find me. The special operations Blackhawks have equipment to allow them to find a radio transmission. Nightstalker's. always the cowboys. This is why everyone in the community loves working with them, as well as their persistence. That's how they earned their nickname N.S.D.Q. Nightstalker's Don't Quit. Chief walker gets his bearings and brings the chopper in low about 30 feet over our heads as he does a fly by. Then, he loops around in a tight circle and flares the chopper so hard for a moment it looks like its vertical. The Flare maneuver is used to scrub the forward speed of the chopper to take it from a rapid speed down to a hover, and this is a violent maneuver. The 160th pilots are adept at these tactical maneuvers. He brings the chopper into a hover over Roscoe and Crash, and they are livid, as the down wash under the chopper at that height is comparable to being trapped in a hurricane. Dusting is what we call it, and Roscoe had this coming as he is always pranking Chief. These two are always going back and forth. Roscoe got Chief on the last op by placing a Tarantula in Chiefs boots. With Chief not liking spiders, this did not play out very well. This tells you that our last op was in South America. We will not elaborate any further as we as professionals and do not speak of these things outside the community. After a good dusting, Doc B does a deep-water entry and swims over to Roscoe. He tells him this was from Chief walker, then swims out to sea as they practice a hoist recovery. Doc B is a task force medic, called thus as a reference to the 160th being initially set up as a task force as they are wrapping things up, they receive a distress call from a fishing boat approximately 100 miles away and do an additional fly by as they go to lend a hand. That is one thing about what we do, routine training can instantly turn into a Real-world situation. We keep our gear and minds sharp and ready at all times.

As I sit and watch all this unfold, I am taken back by the scope of what is going on, I have a job where I get to play with millions of dollars' worth of equipment. How fortunate I am that the government has spent millions just to train us to be able to do this type of work. At times, when I am in the air and I look out at the horizon, fully immersed in the moment, it feels like utter euphoria. The sheer beauty of it all, if only we were a more peace-loving society, then I am transported back to reality as it nears Go Time as we call it. That time where things speed up. It's very odd when I enter this state, it's as if time approaches a standstill, and I process it all at a rapid rate. I can see things approaching before they materialize, like I am hyper aware or omni present.

Angels are shown with swords because the path they take to enlightenment is through physical battle. They must know sometimes it takes the sacrifice of the few to save the many.

THE CRUNCH

As the economy slows down, it seems like the US dollar is not worth the paper they are printing it on. This is mostly in part caused by the US Government and the federal reserve printing 24 trillion dollars during the bail out of 2008. The dollar is hyper inflating so rapidly they are changing the exchange rate for it weekly. There have been mass layoffs and the medical system has taken a huge hit since the rise of Quantum healing. It was demonstrated that our old medical system was merely treating the symptoms, was very corrupt, and now all the oncologists are mostly unemployed as Cancer has been cured, as the people began flocking to these new forms of healthcare, combined with the economy falling, the medical system also came crashing down with weekly layoffs. Nurses don't know if they will get their paychecks or if they will still be employed by the end of the week. Very few doctors are still employed, especially the general practice doctors since there is no money to go to them, and humans learned they can self-heal most of their illness and diseases through Quantum healing and a plant-based diet.

Wall street is nothing but a ghost town. I still remember the traders losing their fortunes, committing suicide by the hundreds, jumping off the same buildings they used to dominate over society, now they are out of time. The suicide rate is insane,we talk about suicides like we used to talk about the weather. It is a dark time, and you can see the stress in the people's faces as they worry about their materiel possessions and where their next meal will come from. Speaking of suicide, the AQHT modality as all but cured suicide, that is if the person wants help to free their minds and to ease their bodies pain.

The housing market saw a huge boom as the people in the north began moving out of the northern parts of North America. After the winter of 2019/2020 it was apparent this region was growing vastly colder. There were massive power outages when houses simply caved in because of the sheer amount of snow that fell on the roofs that were not properly pitched enough to allow the snow and ice to slide off. It was discovered that the older buildings which had steep pitched roofs to allow the snow accumulation to slide off were constructed around the last mini-ice age that had been covered up by the governments, Jesuits and Freemasons after the last reset. The housing market soon failed after the housing prices rose so sharply people could not afford to buy them, nor could they get their money for the houses they had in the norther part of the continent. The normal people began to ask exaggerated prices for anywhere to live in the south. The temperature dropped so low that the homeless froze to death while huddling on the side of the road. There were those that would not allow them inside the buildings in the big cities. But there were also those that took it upon themselves to open their homes and shelters to provide accommodations from the cold that was killing so many. The Evil wind! As I researched, I would often find ancient texts referring to the evil wind, what could they be talking about? So far, we have seen wind so cold it froze the birds in the sky solid as they fell to the earth dead. The ones that did not have a way to heat their homes and stock food simply died from starvation and cold. If they did not starve they become very mineral deficient, this is the real reason I tricked the darkness into Ormus production, the light needed their greed to supply the people with the needed supplement to sustain life. I personally tested ormus while consuming 90 percent processed foods for almost 2 years and my health and vibration stayed extremely high, yet not as high as a plant-based diet. Many were not able to escape their homes from the sheer snowpack and the cold. Cars would not start the roads were un-passable. Many died trying to get to their loved ones. The worst part was the food simply not arriving to the stores. The US has a 3-day supply of food, when the money hyper-inflated the flow of food stopped, the fights and killings that ensued with people fighting over the last scraps like vicious dogs competing over table scraps was utter insanity. People gripped with fear, death and starvation everywhere. People cried out, "If there is a God, how could He let this happen? It's like God is punishing us.... Why?"

The New Earth Emerges!

It is as if some people knew this was coming, there were those that are thriving during these turbulent times. The farmers that moved their growing operations indoors, the inventors that made new inventions to grow food quicker and healthier, the healers that created new ways to heal people without drugs or surgeries, the computer programmers that created wellness websites to bridge the gap between the old 3D world and the New 7D Earth. It is like they couldn't be happier, yet there were others that were in sheer ruin. It is inconceivable how many people were coming together in these smaller communities. They were running their cars and generators off hydrogen from water kits they purchased direct from Amazon and fueled by Ormus, it's a super conductor!

Ormus being paired with anything electrical, batteries and hydrolysis etc. became super charged. All the people that were boycotting amazon were now seeking smaller personal businesses to meet their supply demands.

The rise of the Crypto currency is unfathomable, it seems as if overnight, all the online retailers began accepting these digital currencies. The Crypto scam is a Ponzi gambling scam created by the govt and fueled by scam artists like Jeff Berwick and his Jesuit controller Ed Bugos, this whole scam was to offset the fiat money failure, problem reaction solution. The crypto scam was really a way to pilot test the change into a digital currency. For humanity this is the worst case scenario. In the end it ended up being food that became the next money. Not all crypto currencies are real, most crypto currencies are fake. Crypto comes from the Greek word Kryptos meaning hidden concealed or secret. All the preppers that gambled on the gold and silver to rise to make great gains were in dismay as the metal currency plummeted with the paper dollar. The Light did this to make sure the evil people in power would be left powerless. The elites have run this scam many times before and it was not going to be allowed to play out again. All the elites lost all their acquired wealth, all of it. What didn't hyperinflate was robbed and looted from the people. Karma came back to balance.

The Illuminati unveiled, This organization created the Jesus story.

As the restraints that had been placed on humanity to slow them down from manifesting are removed, they collective moves into self-automation, let me explain! Each human creates their own reality as each human ability to create has been increased, the future of humanity is now being controlled by the people's thoughts. Not prophecy. What we are experiencing in the world is what energies and thoughts people are dealing with. As these parameters are changed, we the people are taking over the reality, that we the people are experiencing. This takes a while for the people to see this and to adapt to it, at first the darkness lies as always and takes full credit for everything with their propaganda and their hypnosis brainwashing taking credit for all that is revealed and exposed. These are energy traps to get people upset and into the fear and anger mode, the darkness does this to harvest this energy for its own purposes. It is a magical battle out there with two separate forces Love Vs Evol battling at every turn, each battle just as important as each decision that we make is. We live in a time where ONE decision can change your entire timeline you will experience. I strongly urge people to evaluate each decision you make, using love as your guide, is this decision for your highest good First? Next is this decision for the highest good of all parties it will affect? If yes, then continue. If no, then you should reevaluate.

THE OTHER SIDE
OF THE COIN

There are retreats set up all over the world that seemingly materialize out of thin air. Then you have the healers that set them up as 3 to 5-day retreats and they teach people how to selfheal from hypnosis and energy healing but most importantly they are taught about a plant based non processed diet, let food be thy medicine! The masses are taught the truth of reality to replace the old 3D programming. It seems insane that we live more in touch with nature as our technology has increased greatly. The retreats consist of living a simpler life while enjoying the amazing new technologies that are rolling out. These people are so happy, centered and grounded and the chaos all around them does not affect them. We travel around teaching the others our ways, The survivors of Atlantis have woken! We teach them how to live their lives in the same fashion, although for some, it is not retained. They refuse to live this way as they liked the old way. These people go off in groups armed with their guns and prepper stock food. These people do not make it but a short time living like this. Only the ones that come together will make it through this. There is no way anyone could prep enough supplies to last eighty years.

Living away from the cities was a godsend for us, we were far enough away yet close enough if we needed to go into town, we could reach it within an hour. The turmoil, riots and marshal law do not affect us, and no one cares what we are doing out here.

As we travel and get into pockets of people that are expecting the worst, we show and teach them that each human generates their own reality. After learning this, they understand that it makes no sense for them to create an end of days experience for themselves. Most change their thinking patterns and begin creating heaven on earth for themselves, 7D!

The life we are now living is like that of an advanced civilization. I have an electric hover bike that will fly for an hour before needing recharging, which can be done from an old 120-volt receptacle or a 12v source. It also has a solar option, but that takes half the day with good sunshine to charge. We do not get much sunshine these days, The vulcanization of the upper atmosphere from all the volcanoes going off, cools the planet. I also have a hover car or pod. It's completely enclosed and autonomous. It will fly for 3 hours straight and has a parachute safety system. It operates at a higher altitude of 1500 ft which is a little higher than the hover bike. We still have regular cars as well, although they run on hemp gas or hydrogen instead of regular fuel. Living life this way is amazing and we are so much happier than we ever were before. This life has meaning, this life has purpose. The best experience is pulling stragglers out of the old paradigm system when they arrive at one of our tiny house villages. Seeing these people transition into a state of oneness and happiness is the greatest feeling I have ever experienced in any lifetime I have ever lived. The way we live now is the way humans were meant to live. We live in oneness and harmony with nature and each other as we heal

Gaia. As we take care of her and her systems, the trees and water systems, we celebrate the oneness between the human and Gaia and Source.

Yet we all know that there is a day of sorrow coming. It is that day when the two worlds, the two very different vibrations will separate and not be accessible anymore. The day of the rapture is drawing ever closer, and we feel it!

The day of this separation is much sought after as well as well guarded. Maybe the most guarded secret ever known to mankind. Known to only one entity. The Creator herself is here to handle this personally, it is her and only her that will handle this as she has trusted others to complete this mission several times before only to go through the evolution reset process only to find the scourge of darkness following the light through the transition as if they knew it was coming? They did know, it was this secret that was leaked from whatever source it leaked from that allowed darkness to take over the earth. Draconian's are astral beings and presently way more evolved than humans, the Draco's have been manipulating the human dna for 2k years now. It is for this reason the creator is here herself to handle this herself. When she decides she has had enough she will trigger the separation. She was very solid here on the explanation as well as the delivery. She clearly stated that she judges instantly if the soul she is in contact with is worth saving and letting it evolve. She stated that she comes into contact with these people then judges them as a whole if they are conscious enough to evolve further. She also stated her sadness that many here are unworthy of evolution. It is funny as I have told others about this, they are upset that there is someone here judging them. This blows my mind as clearly there is a plan guided by a higher power, why wouldn't our creator judge us on our performance? I would. Had I been the creator that created all this. Its common sense really!

The Lion of Judah is the demi urge!

THE GREAT DECEPTION

The coming great Deception will include the darkness making use of the secret technologies they have hidden from humanity for over 7 decades in order to carry out the largest deception of mankind. I recently read Sir Francis Bacons New Atlantis, its marked as a utopian novel but really it was a statement of things to come and the state of the freemasons or the House of Solomona as it's referred to in the book. If you read it he tells us the current America was the capitol of Atlantis and that in the early 1600s the freemasons, the Draconian's live in massive cities under the earth, some as deep as 3 miles as well they brag about the technology they have acquired that's hidden from humanity, and that they have people that they send out to collect the new technologies that humans create. As always, there is always some truth mixed in with deception to make it resonate with the humans, but it is always 180 degrees backwards. Using this backwards principle, we have been able to decode a variety of plans and deceptions they have concocted. The fake alien agenda a counterfeit and man-made alien spacecraft can only be used in our atmosphere. In Project Bluebeam, they took their holographic technology to the highest level, and they have used and tested it many times over to see how well it would work and what the reaction to it would be. The Reptilian lead Nazi Freemasons are the ones responsible for creating and hiding the flying saucer technology. This plan was put into effect amplified by the Order of the eastern star and Dolores Cannon. She claims gave us the modality of past life regression; Dolores having stolen the techniques of Edgar Cayce. The darkness used the entities that are attached to manipulate the information that comes out of the sessions. These entities have the ability to manipulate the visualization and emotional part of the past life regression, this is why she puts it first in her modality. To support and create the alien agenda. This is why she forbid any of her students from speaking of entities.

This is also why her crony Candice also forbade anyone from speaking of these things as well. Clearly an agenda here!

The entities do work with the darkness in general, but they can also be commanded to attach and manipulate humans. This is called conjuring. With this deception, they will fool the majority of humans who know Aliens are real. They simply do not understand that the aliens are us in the human avatar. This is also why when I began exposing these things, Candice had to ban me from her site, or I was rapidly proving that the QHHT and BQH modalities are dangerous and have nasty effects on real light workers, a real light worker will have had a massive life of traumas, the older souls have the hardest lives! . The play is ever so simple and was created long ago during WW2 with the Nazi and American forces pretending to be at war yet secretly working together. The Antarctic expeditions containing falsified information spread about alien technology to hide the fact that the earth is flat, and Antarctica is the edge. They must convince the general population that they live on a spinning ball and that the humans can leave the physical earth. They had to hide intelligent design, if the earth is a flat plane and has edges it's clearly a created construct from a higher intelligence. They were clearly trying to see if they could break free from the earths containment system with Operation High Jump. Operation Fishbowl followed, which was clearly testing the limits of the "fishbowl" we reside in. Now that they know the truth, they must hide this from the humans. If the humans found out that they lived in an enormous fishbowl they would understand that everything was created just for them. That would provide them with clear evidence of a Creator. In order to keep Draconian control of the slaves they use to build their machines and to try to break free of the Earths dome, a deception must be created. NASA is that deception which is one of the most Reptilian Freemason organizations on the planet. And YOU funded it, 600 billion dollars of taxpayer money has been given to them. A google search of NASA Freemasons will show they are all Freemasons, and all the missions are branded with occulted names and agendas. Occult means secret or hidden. The secret agenda is hatched and the powers that be use war along with the Reptilian controlled media to keep this false paradigm alive. A simple search of the countries that have signed the Antarctic treaty is a list of Draconian controlled countries, there are 195 official countries listed, 54 countries have signed it, these of course are the bigger countries.

Do you ever wonder why every news station is surrounded by walls and gates, like it's a prison? They cannot have you coming around asking questions! These TV stations are their control of humanity, you see the only way to force hypnosis is to do it with the eyes wide open.

The Draconian's and the elite have spent so much time, money and effort preparing for their grand deception. You paid for it with 600 billion of your dollars used to lie and mislead you. Touché NASA. Touché

They upscaled their operation by pretending to create a space force for defense followed by a false flag attack destroying the fake space station. It was only smoke and mirrors as is clearly proven on YouTube showing wires getting caught in the footage and exposed as well as the numerous Freemason hand signals of their fake video live feeds from space. They followed it up with advanced laser technology to attack various cities. The James Webb telescope is a laser DEW weapon they will deploy soon to attack the humans and pretend it was ALIENS. The resemblance of the James Webb telescope to the nasa sun simulator is crazy. The test run for this new laser technology was rolled out in California as well as the deep-water horizon rig prior to the oil spill. The reason behind the massive oil spill was to change the ocean current to keep cooler water from entering the gulf to try to push back the onset of the ice age.

The State controlled media then began running V.N. R's. These are video news releases that are made and packaged by the government and then shipped to news stations who then air them as real-life events. President Draco Reptilian Bush Jr explains this to a reporter in a YouTube video and he says it is not us it is the D.O.J., the department of justice who says they are constitutional. The Freemasons are masters at blaming another part of their own organization. This is done purposely and called plausible deniability. President Bush is knighted by the Draco Reptilian Queen following his presidency. His Grandfather Prescot Bush was tried in US courts for supplying money to Hitler during WW2 ultimately funding the people that were killing our grandparents.

After the movies of aliens attacking humans, this deception was easy to pull off.

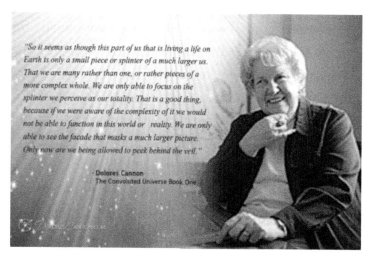

"So it seems as though this part of us that is living a life on Earth is only a small piece or splinter of a much larger us. That we are many rather than one, or rather pieces of a more complex whole. We are only able to focus on the splinter we perceive as our totality. That is a good thing, because if we were aware of the complexity of it we would not be able to function in this world or reality. We are only able to see the facade that masks a much larger picture. Only now are we being allowed to peek behind the veil."

- Dolores Cannon
The Convoluted Universe Book One

Note the devil horns hand sign.

There are three planes of causation: the physical, the spiritual and the mental. This is the story of how they carried out this great deception on the spiritual plane.

Dolores bringing out past life regression before the light accomplished two things. It gave the darkness the ability to frame the environment, the Alien agenda the ability to hide entity attachments which virtually every human has, and the ability to attack lightworkers. Let me elaborate on this, an older soul that comes to earth will not take an easy life sitting in a mansion on a hill with barely any struggles. An older soul or lightworker comes here to be challenged. Yes, to be raped, molested, beaten and thrown into prison. etc. Knowing these things from Dolores doing her own past life regressions, they gave us past life regression backwards. In the QHHT method, they do the visualization first. This puts that older soul at a high risk of attack during the session by one of the attached entities! Or the Freemasons and O.E.S. have conjured up to be attached, as was in the case of my ex-wife and me. These things can and do make their host think things that are not their thoughts as well as to feel emotions that do not belong to them. Dolores knew this would happen because she fills two pages in her course on how to calm down a client after they have freaked out. They can manipulate their host so easily its insane. My research has proven this without a doubt. I no longer practice the QHHT method as it is outdated and dangerous for the client. It provides no physical healing for the client. Each one of the practitioners who has a client that goes berserk will have to answer for their actions. There are many dark workers in the field of past life regression. Ask to see their own regression video before ever allowing one of them to do a regression on you, and make sure you do a Advanced Quantum Healing Technique Healing session before doing any past life regression. All entities on the earth plane make quick use of the portal I created with this healing modality i opened for them as well as the Reptilians and Grays who are enslaved by the Draconian's. They quickly begin telling a story of a galactic war and the so-called Federation of Light to create an alternate timeline. This timeline has several functions, one of which is to convince the humans to create an energy source for them to escape from the enclosed Earth plane. The Earth is Quarantine for the darkness that is here. If it were to get out it, would cause massive destruction and will never be allowed. Secondly, to create the idea in the human mind that the aliens are something separate from themselves. When the Galactic's come into our materiel existence to help, the humans will be in fear. With the Draconian control system, it is all about fear. Through mind programming, they keep the human in a constant state of fear, triggering them when they want or need the fear energy. They then use that fear energy to create or to control.

The darkness has gone to great lengths with their secret alien technology which they keep hidden from the public eye. They created constant mind programming, poisons and chemicals in the food and water and the use of religion to back up the earth realm with entities, all to hide the Creator from them. With secret societies controlling all governments and the use of dark magic, there is not one system they have not convoluted. Clinton, how are we to overcome these odds? First off, rest easy the Light has already won. Rejoice in love knowing the light cannot be stopped from freeing this planet. We effectively have come from the future to save humanity. The Earth was created for the light to learn how to shine. It's the garden of Eden and it is once again open! The Darkness thought it could keep us separated but this was not true, they thought they could slow the rate at which light took over, and again they were mistaken.

At this time, the darkness is petrified and is in a major defensive posture. Many are now realizing they have lost!

I recently had the first Freemason come get healed and rescind his oath.

The battle plan is very easy to understand, each client that we heal we raise up to a higher timeline, they ascend, really their ability to learn and re program their mind is all that stops them from living any life they want. By self-healing we are able to affect multiple timelines and entire families. Mother and children's lives are raised up and brought out of chaos and back into a loving balance, lives lived without pain, without the heart ache from the past traumas. Healed forever by healing the energy that was underlying. Husbands and wives that were at odds are once again able to find the love that brought them together in the first place. Families able to manifest their desires with no more obstacles. The affect removing these energetic attachments have been absolutely amazing to the spiritual and physical health of the human. These are the cause for all disease and illness. When we combine this Quantum Healing with the modern allopathic medicine also combined with plant-based medicine, we will greatly extend human life here on earth. We have already had great success in curing cancer, auto immune disease, herpes, aids, Lyme disease, and yes autism which is caused by the heavy metals in the injections. No one should ever get an injection. This blows my mind here our creator can make this world, these bodies and every single thing here yet too stupid to make an immune system? This was the reason that they had to hide intelligent design, raise up the view of man's intelligence as its more than it really is. Man's intelligence and the paid for science is very lacking in all aspects.

First Contact

As individuals heal themselves and healers' step into their power in healing the collective, the vibrations of those individuals begin to rise. Together as a collective we are raising our vibrations. Meanwhile, the Earth is traveling deeper and deeper into the age of light which means we are getting ever closer to the central sun or Source itself, the Light that permeates everything. Everything on earth is being infused with higher waves of love energy. This is what is what is heightening the second coming of Christ, The Christ (Christ means messenger) consciousness is coming to all, only incarnated energies cam affect this realm with any great impact. The Christ or messenger of the age is incarnated now. whether they like it or not. Everything will be assimilated, organizations that were once very dark will change overnight and transition into organizations of light and good. The dark aspects will be thrust into the Light for all to see, nothing will be hidden during this time. Everything will run to the light. This is why the field of Quantum Healing will be one of the most abundant on the planet. We are the doctors of the future. They pay us to keep them healthy, which is opposite of the old paradigm of getting sick from dis-ease and then paying someone to try to restore their health.

This is the story of what it was like to live this time and to experience the changes in the physical realm.

Adam has 3 days left of his R&R when his telepager goes off. This is the way the special operations forces are alerted when needed. It's like a texting cell satellite phone but it doesn't make or accept calls, our electric leash if you will. This is a level 1 alert which means without a doubt it's a real-world situation. The level 2 alerts can be training or can turn into a real-world alert, and level 3 alerts are training alerts. Level 3's are the worst as we might get to the airfield and then go home, or we might load up everything and fly away to do a training operation for a unknown time. As we arrive at the airfield, there are more black hawks with rotors turning than I have ever seen, as well as many ospreys. Something big is going on. Adam reports to Roscoe who arrives in shorts and flippers, looking like he drove straight from the beach, this guy always the comedian. As Roscoe begins to disseminate the known information, it is in great awe that I receive the relayed information. We are going to provide medical support for a massive "snatch and grab" as we call it. My mind is having trouble comprehending this situation. The entire assortment of special operations force is mobilized.

There has been a shutdown of the Federal government and all the politicians are ordered to be arrested. This is done with the Convention of the States. A back door if things ever got out of control. Like right now. Though we don't know why, we follow through with our orders as this is what a soldier's life consists of. My team leader says go... and I go. After being in combat many times and Roscoe saving my life more times than I care to admit, I trust this man with my life. Our op order is to provide CSAR support. CSAR is combat search and rescue which is our specialty.

This is what a PJ was created for. This is what we live for. There is not a PJ alive that is not an adrenaline junkie. It is like it permeates every cell of our being. The Door kickers as we call them, the operators that are trained and tasked to go in and get the HVT or high value target are all here, delta, SF teams, and the special forces A and B teams. These are 12-man teams that do small team missions. Rangers from the Ranger Battalions which are Army soldiers that are the infantry of special operations. A 90 percent loss rate is acceptable in their operation parameters. They are highly motivated and many of the operators start out from the Ranger battalions. They will be very quick to tell you that just because a soldier is wearing a Ranger tab on his shoulder, it does not mean he's special operator. That soldier is only Ranger qualified as they put it, if they have been assigned to a Ranger Battalion. Everyone is loading up gear and loading weapons. I have never seen anything like this.

Roscoe comes back from the command meeting with our combat controller, CCT for short, who we know from prior missions. CCT's are the air traffic controllers on the ground and arrange our fire support from the air force and different special forces. They speak their own language which pilots understand. We call him WIFI as he can always seem to get us internet from anywhere on the planet, as well as our TACP or tactical Air control party, which are the liaisons between the Army and Airforce.

This operation is serious, and for a moment the fear creeps in as I acknowledge and then deal with it. When I move on, I am reminded that if you did not fear the many unknowns that are coming, you wouldn't belong in this business. This is the difference between us and the rest. We acknowledge the fear, overcome it and move forward.

As we board our Osprey and take off, we are headed north up the coast to take up our station route for our CSAR mission. We do a refueling operation just before we get to our station coordinates which puts us around the Virginia and West Virginia border. We have teams that are going into DC as well as West Virginia at the Greenbrier Resort. As the operation kicks off, every politician is now under arrest, and we are now hunting the same people that used to send us to other countries to fight on their behalf. The magnitude of this is mind blowing. I try to push the thought of it into the background as the radio starts to pick up as the operation is now well underway. The teams that went into the white house to secure the President have meet with resistance and there have been casualties. They are a secondary mission for us as our primary is the recovery of downed aircraft personnel, and so far, so good let's keep it this way. I do believe in the power of good intention.

No sooner than this thought goes through my head, we receive the call. Black hawk down, the coordinates put it at the Greenbrier hotel. We climb to an altitude of 10k feet and rig inflight. We will do a Halo jump which is a high altitude, low opening jump. We will jump in to access the situation and then bring in follow up resources as is safe and needed. This LZ is considered a hot LZ, LZ is military for landing zone, Hot means that there is too much combat to risk putting a million dollar aircraft into the area.

As we approach our jump point, I can feel my heartbeat in my throat and my mouth dries up. This is from the adrenaline rush. I remove my mouthpiece from my camelback and take a swig of water. This is a water bladder that we wear on our back. It fits into a specially designed pouch. This always helps. For some strange reason I have a feeling that life will never be the same again. The ramp at the back comes open and makes a sucking sound like you never will understand unless you have been in an airplane at high speeds while it depressurizes. This being a high-altitude jump, we do have our O2 set ups on. We light our IR chemlights which are infrared glow sticks that can only be seen with aided night vision.

The jump master does his checks, and we receive the 1-minute sign which is a finger pointing straight up. This is followed by the 30 second sign which is two fingers, the thumb and forefinger held close together. Then Roscoe leads us out the back with a backflip, this guy! The jump was remarkable just as any other. Our deployment altitude is 3k feet and as our chutes deploy this gives us a little buffer as the terrain is about 2k feet above sea level, I look around and count 1..2..3..4..5..6, ok everyone is accounted for. What a picture-perfect jump. I take up following Roscoe as we descend. I know it's him as he has approximately 50 chemlights on his rig. Roscoe looks like a flying Christmas tree.

As we approach the target area, all hell is breaking loose. This is definitely a hot landing zone. Apparently, we were expected. I can see bullets being fired on the ground and in the air as well as some other kind of laser type weapon and some other kind of pulse weapon. Who the hell are we fighting here? Roscoe takes us in through a Valley and into the side of a mountain about a kilometer from the objective. I manage to miss a huge tree and brush by it as I land sideways into this mountain, knocking the breath out of my lungs. I gather my gear, hide my chute and deploy my weapon while I situate myself and establish communications. With spartan 6, this is Roscoe, the 6 is always the leader. I am spartan 1 as I am the newest member of the team. We link up at the edge of a clearing and survey the situation. The radio is a buzz of orders and people calling for medevac and fire support. Medevac is medical evacuation. There is no way we are going to be able to bring aircraft into this situation, we will have to establish fire superiority before we can evacuate the patients elsewhere to set up a casualty collection point or CCP as we call it. Roscoe moves us out in single file towards the target area. We see fires burning and the smell of jet fuel as we move very cautiously towards our objective, the downed helicopter. As we get about 1000 meters from the aircraft, we see tracers and light beams shooting in all directions. What kind of weapons are these and who are we fighting? This is insanity, like something out of a science fiction movie. My mind is having a hard time comprehending this scene.

Roscoe sees me staring with my mouth wide open and hits me in the shoulder. He reminds me to get in the game and to focus, our objective is no different this day than any other. We start bounding in two-man fire teams, one covering and the other moving. As we use smoke canisters as concealment to move forward. As we near the aircraft, we begin taking effective fire at close range. You can tell the difference by the whistle the bullet makes as it breaks the sound barrier zooming by your head. I drop down and start low crawling into the crash site as I call out the friendly ID of "friendly," and the code "Billy had a lil goat," and their reply is "to the moon." This lets us know who is a friendly and who is not, as our enemy is dressed in the same gear as us. As I drag myself up to a car mangled from the impact of the chopper, I recognize Doc B from the 160th. SOAR. He looks like hammered dung warmed in the microwave. I try to say something comical, but all that comes out is "hey buddy!" He says, "I got 2 kia and two urgent surgical." And I say, "hey buddy, do you know you're bleeding?" He looks down and nearly passes out as Doc B realizes it's his own blood all over his lower pant leg. I sit him down and cut open his pant leg. He has a piece of some kind of metal protruding from his calf. Knowing my anatomy from cutting down cadavers in S.O.M.C., the special operations medical course, I grab some hemostats, pull the shrapnel out and put a pressure dressing on it. Our team moves without speaking as we have practiced so many times before in training and in other missions. This is not our first time being under fire.

We are elite for a reason; we are efficient at what we do. We are trauma gods. Roscoe moves with Wi-Fi and the Tacp guy who is new to us, and they begin accessing the situation, putting down covering fire and calling in fire support. Around the same time, the sky becomes very dark. I see a stream of bullets with similarity to lasers as Wi-Fi places the fire where it is needed from the Spectre gunship doing its pilon turn at 10k feet above our heads. It is so high it is impossible to see with the naked eye. This brings the amount of fire we are receiving down dramatically. The SF teams move on the position the Specter just pounded. As the SF team prepares to assault the position, a 160th DAP direct action penetrator comes in with a 7.62 mini gun and 30mm for the objective. When the 160th gunships fire, it is so close above your head that hot brass often rains down on our heads, we all have nasty burn scars from this. It is better than being dead. Then the SF team takes the objective which is in the front of the Greenbrier hotel. The call over the radio will never escape my memory, "These things are not human," clarification is requested from higher up as well as video confirmation. It is clearly said that they look like us, but their heads are different, and they look reptilian as their eyes are different. At this time, Roscoe comes across our radio telling us to focus on our task. I get the first patient and he has a gaping hole through his jaw, gasping for air. I do a Cricothyroidotomy or a Cric as we call it, to establish his airway. He is still having issues breathing and spitting blood out of his Cric, so I get my stethoscope out listen to his lungs. Precisely what I suspected; he has a hemo/Pneumothorax. I ready a chest tube and tell him, "Bro this is going to hurt." He is barely conscious, but from experience he will feel this. I locate the position, make my cut between the ribs and insert the tube. He groans in pain, even immediately before death, they always feel this procedure. I reassure him it will be all right and he will not be dying today, nobody dies on me! I secure the Hemothorax and administer morphine and write on his forehead with my sharpie. I continue my assessment and find a few other minor bleeds before packing him up for transport. About this time, we are told the beings have retreated into the underground bunker. We call in medevac. As the 160th chopper pulls into its flare and drops the hoist, they tell us they do not have a medic on board. Roscoe tells me to ride transport. I ride the winch up first and then we winch the other patients up. After they are all onboard, we are off towards the CCP, the casualty collection point. We have some very modified C17 Globemasters that end up as a traveling surgical center. They are set up on a nearby airfield about 30 minutes flight at full speed. As we touch down, I turn my patients over to the surgical teams. I wash up and take a moment to process what just happened. As I am sitting outside, a soldier walks up and asks if I want a cigarette, I say "yes please," but I do not smoke.

The human race is not alone here. This changes everything.

MY DECENT INTO THE UNDERWORLD {DUAT}

In 2012 I went through a spiritual awakening and did not understand how the world, I lived in changed so drastically and seemingly overnight, little did I know it would take 6 years to understand what had actually happened!

The reality of what happened was that I descended to the lowest vibrational reality in existence. It was not all at once. I look back, I was slipping down over the years. Timeline after timeline, until I reached the bottom timeline, all this leading up to the year 2012. The final drop was certainly in 2012 and was enough to make it a noticeable event. The first reaction was shock, "Where the hell am I and how did this happen?" How did I end up in a world so backwards? I would come to understand later that the actions taken by the darkness had much to do with this as well the actions of 911. The twin towers event had a tremendous amount to do with it. You see, anytime they create a high death and war toll or poverty, it lowers the collective conscious vibration, any time you see massive poverty or war our Realm controllers are trying to bring down the collective vibration. This makes us controllable, physical slaves that they can easily manipulate and controlled. This is one of the reasons the Freemasons use the number 33. If they can keep our consciousness under that percentage, they have secured their slaves. This is one of the reasons there is so much created scarcity and poverty exist here on earth. As we share, give and care for each other, we are taking the blocks out of the prison walls the darkness has built to enslave humanity. A slave construct, this construct it is nothing more than a simulation that our consciousness experiences in a biomechanical avatar, The Matrix was a documentary!

A side note!

As I write this, I receive a call from a California number. It is a well-recognized movie headhunter scouting new books for upcoming movie ideas. He says he's interested, and I tell him I have book two almost completed. He asks if I would be willing to fly out to California and have a meeting. Why yes, I would love to! Two days later I am on a private jet flying nonstop to Hollywood where they put me and my service dog Triton up at a house in the LA hillside with a spectacular view.

The next day at the meeting, a deal is struck, and they buy the rights to the New Earth series for print and movie rights. A cool Fifty million and the standard 15 percent royalties. As I sign the deal, the money is wired into my account within the hour, End zone dance! I am speechless. I am made to sign a non-disclosure act as I cannot tell who is making the movies until they break it to the press. I am however allowed to say there has been a deal made!

I know now that as we raise our individual vibrations, we carry more light. Each time we give unconditionally, or we help another in need, these acts of love enable us to carry more light. That light we carry raises the vibration of the collective and wakes up much more people. You see, I see all these people on social media posting things and trying to bring things into the light, or truth. The real fact is that it mostly hurts because each human generates their own reality. Everything they see and hear whether they consciously know it or not. They are manifesting what they see and hear into existence, and this is absolutely known and used against the population. Sadly, all this must happen to awaken humanity. All these people trying to help are really hurting. As others and I begin putting this information out and begin only posting about the things that we want to see in the world, then it begins changing that world. We are all co creating the collective reality. After the 144000 begins doing this as a whole, we start pacing the social media. As we are all so much more connected now, it spread like wildfire. We take the upper hand from the darkness that created these venues to control and pace us. The tide has turned towards the love.

As of my most recent sessions, the information is that we are doing an excellent job comes through.

We are defeating the darkness and they are on the defensive. They are afraid and beginning to see they have already lost, and it cannot be stopped. Most of the high-level Jesuits along with the Skull and Bones are attempting to hide out in their secret islands. The Draconian's that are controlling everything are trying to figure out a way to leave and go to Mars. A new planet to enslave! Therefore, you hear them conversing about going to mars on TV. These are Draconian's trying to create a way to escape the coming of the light. They will never be allowed to leave and will be given the opportunity to turn to the love before being recycled to the central sun.

There are waves of light and energy steadily hitting the Earth as we ascend. These waves serve many purposes. They reset the old control systems and flush out negative energies that are present inside the humans. They will have to first self-heal, which is only good up to a point, then they will need to find a healer.

The Creator has designed this realm to operate this way, we must work together to heal!

These healers are usually AQHT practitioners as AQHt is the pinnacle of healing on this planet at this time, presently we have 5 years of quantum research to support our techniques but there are others that can-do similar healing methods. The AQHT practitioners are the most advanced at this point, and there is not even a close second currently. Therefore, we are so busy and booked out so far. These light waves are raising the vibration of the collective at a steady rate and one that will be optimal for the collective. This action alone causes many to recycle as many souls are not a vibrational match to the higher vibrations and many choose to help from the other side. This is why there are so many people dying from random illnesses. The truth is that they are just not a vibrational match.

We either match the energy that is incoming or we too will die!

The Darkness will come up with some excuse to cover up these ascension deaths, most likely a virus as that's their normal response from the ascensions in the past.

The ascended experts along with other Lightworkers doing collective work to transmute energies held in Gaia as well as in the aether, we as a whole are raising the vibration at such a rapid rate the darkness cannot keep up with it. We are linked to one another and us the lightworkers are doing the heavy lifting for the sleepwalking collective.

Rest easy love Warriors, we are victorious. The day of evolution comes closer every second, but we have all the time that is needed to not feel rushed. Make sure to take care of yourselves. The mission we are carrying out is very important and it is equally important that we help each other and take care of ourselves. You are Victorious! I am so proud of each and every one of you and grateful to all who have stepped forward to lead this Ascension. There will be a new time marker set in the future as we EVOLVE humanity to the galactic level. This is the marker that all races from the stars pass as a graduation point. Earth and the humans have done this in record time. As a collective, we worked together at a level of efficiency that has set the standard for all to benchmark the ascension of this race to the Galactic level.

LOVE AND LIGHT TO ALL!

Zinaru!

Note

As I write this our world is now forever changed. People will read these words and will wake up to the fact that many have known about these times and what would happen as we navigate our way through this wrinkle in time. Many are waking up to the fact that they lived in a fake world made up of lies and fear. Many are waking up to the fact that we are definitely not alone here and never have been.

We all are waking up to the fact that we each carry a light inside us. A light that is nothing but love and healing!

A light that connects us each to the other!

We are all one!

Its only together we rise!

ASCENSION ADDENDUM

At the time of the original writing spirit would not let me release the parameters that all would have to conform to be able to ascend to the higher world. With much joy and gratitude, I am now allowed to release this information. When I asked why I could not release this information I was told that darkness is watching these books and will make their plans by the words that I write, they told me that many false prophets would arise to deceive the masses! And holy cow where they right! As soon as Ascension was released a hoard of influencers started preaching their ascend to 5D trick, you see we are going to 7D not 5D, in Hermetics 5 means scarcity and male, it also means physical changes manifesting into the physical reality. Draconian's are beings from the 5th dimension, they live in this realm by soul possession and after their time here will be returning to the 5th dimension or be destroyed and recycled to the central sun. Ascend to 5 D is a dark trap to get people to manifest their non ascension. You see its all free will and the Draco's manipulate this with their massive propaganda machines. In Hermetics 7 means divine, we are all going to the garden of Eden or you're going back to source. This is not a punishment its simple energy, the energy we are in will keep raising for the next 6k years. Earth has never been into this energy with humans on the planet. This energy is so high it is killing all that do not match the incoming energy, example if you eat meat you're eating the vibration of death, you will too die of cancers, {it was just passed on to me recently the meat has now been cursed, when u eat the vibration of death you too will get sick and die very rapidly} if you do not have love in your heart you will die very very fast, ask my father Clint Sr., never have I felt more hatred in a human's heart, even when dealing with demons. He died of lung cancer from a nasty attachment attached there and his constant eating of flesh. All this was designed by the Divine so humanity could be saved and evolved with very little fighting, to take this world back all we got to do is embody love for all beings. The Nephilim will not be here after this flood, they must eat meat to stay in our vibration, they are being starved to death presently. At the time I did not really believe this, but wow was I in for a huge awakening! One very dark draconian told me she read over 400 books looking for me. Darkness knows I always write books to disseminate info and to lead those to ascension. At the current time of writing this the entire world has erupted into chaos, Kazakhstan has now fallen, the people revolted against the Draconian oppressors over jibby jab passports. The Draconian's control the mainstream media and are reporting that this happened over the price of heating oil, which is also true but leaves out the real cause. In 24 hours, the countries government has either fled or been arrested including the police and military, all vaccination sites were stormed by the people, arresting the Drs and staff present, the government buildings set ablaze. The Humans on earth standing up to their enslavers with a loud resounding NO! we will not accept this oppression anymore! It was very funny for me to read the reviews of the first writing of this book, dark workers angry the book did not contain the parameters of this ascension. This day it will be released. The Virus the Draconian's are battling is love. Love is the virus to their slave matrix. A construct that only exists in the minds of the brainwashed humans. The Earth is in spiritual warfare, the divine will make you use your free will to choose a side. Not picking is choosing a side!

Ascension, what is it? Ascension is clearly shown throughout time and antiquity as a time on earth when a window is opened for mass ascension to gain access to higher vibrating realities to live in, it's all individual, the mass awakening is when the spiritual battle spills into the physical realm and that time is now. When the shelves in the stores have no food, when there is the mark of the beast jibby jab passport required to enter buildings or to shop or to access their banking accounts. The banking access is what set off the revolution in Kazakhstan. The US is already trying to mitigate this by requiring all banking personnel now to work remotely claiming some new variant outbreak. They think it will save lives and it will, the banks in Kazakhstan all were immediately robbed and the personnel arrested and imprisoned. The only way we know this information is because of odysee.com a blockchain technology where anything can be uploaded with no censorship except the kind that should be in place like no pedophilia etc. the Facebook and YouTube platforms are Draconian controlled and are being abandoned at a huge rate due to the censorship and shadow banning.

NOTE

In WW2 the Nazi are the Draconian's. These two terms can be used in unison both are speaking to the same being's structure organization and purpose.

Ascension is the time when the wheat is separated from the shaft. Mathew 3:12, Gather his wheat into the garner, but he will burn up the chaff with unquenchable fire! This means that all that do not make the spiritual weight {lightness} required for ascension will be destroyed by being judged and reclaimed into source, the unquenchable fire! 80 percent of all beings here do not make it, meat eating is the main cause, the second is not having love for all beings. These two issues really are tied together as if you love animals and have love for all beings you would not support anything regarding their enslavement and enslavement and torture. 95 percent of all animals on this planet are enslaved. 60 percent of all pollution comes from AG farming. The plants and water that's used to raise and grow the meats that eaten could easily feed and water every human on this planet x2. How selfish are you to eat that meat? Is it so important to starve people in other areas for it? To destroy the earth? to destroy animals.?

Any megalith with ascending stairs is a testament to the ascension process here on earth.

We see here the Freemason are well aware of the ascension process here as well.

This ascension is the most important event in all our lives, these fake spirituality preachers say you are eternal, this is true to a point, darkness always tells a little truth in their lie's so it will resonate, please let me explain how it pertains here. We are all eternal in the respect as long as we do not sell our soul to the Draconian's via a soul contract or oath. { I have seen a couple of these, they have very few words , mostly lines of numbers with words mixed into them, when a person signs this they agree to serve their new master that gave them the contract} The light we carry is eternal, not as john or betty or mike, this light is eternal to source, if at the time of ascension, if you do not ascend it is because we are judged and if our soul is not found worthy it is recycled, This happens at the end of every cycle, that person will never be an individual creator being ever again, their energy will be transmuted to form a planet or a rock. Some very dark souls will get torture then eternal death. The only way to ascend is through Jesus! Hermetically this translates the only way to ascend is through Zeus healing modality and to enter Eden through Arc Angel Uriel, this is the same being as Thoth from Atlantis as well as Zeus.

Note

The letter J didn't exist 400 years ago, the letter J is a new creation to hide the Messiahs true name, so the saviors name could not be Jesus. I will cover this later in my autobiography on the secret doctrine. There up to this point has always been two doctrines, one for the masses that are not ready or would use this knowledge to cause strife and the secret doctrine known only to the elect adepts and the dark masters. Jesus real name in that life was ilesus. This was also done to protect the messiah until the time of the final battle.

These souls that are incarnated here were chosen from trillions to be allowed to incarnate. Why incarnate? As a being of light, we are do not feel anything but varying forms of love. A fast track to evolve we incarnate into these avatar bodies on this realm and zillions of other realms as we physically feel the responses to our decisions and the environment, we learn very fast thus fast tracking our soul's evolution on our journey back to source. Ascension is graduation time on earth. You can ignore it but the only way to experience heaven on earth and to become eternal is to ascend! The only way out is up!

This ascension is particularly the most special ascension ever on this planet. This type of ascension is a worldwide reset, the evolution of humanity. This ascension will mark the end of darkness! Thoth told us long ago that there is a time in the future when all will become light. this time is upon us. Darkness likes to point out that without them{ego} this could not happen. The truth is the total earth was at the garden of Eden vibration and was already here, and darkness destroyed it trying to build their new world order, I say build because a mason builds and that's what they have done here a spoon fool at a time. I relate it to this saying: to cook a frog alive we just slowly turn up the heat, by the time the frog gets uncomfortable, the heat has already cooked the internals and the frog cannot jump out. This is actually how love defeated the dark, by making the dark show its hand way too soon! The more darkness locks down the people, the more segregation, the forced injections the faster the people are waking up and standing up for freedom! This ascension is at the end of a cycle{the Mayan calendar was correct} this time we are in is called the rift in time and it lasts for a very short time{which spirit will not allow me to reveal} this rift in time is fast coming to a close, when it ends the ascension is over and the old world, that 3d world we came from and all those that did not ascend will be judged and ascended or destroyed, some souls will not be destroyed or recycled but they will have to wait thousands of years before they will match the vibration to be able to incarnate on earth again. This ascension is also timed with the ice age, this ice age is how Gaia restores the earth's resources for the new cycle. The earth is also switching polarities, let me explain this as the humans are being told the negative pole of earth will become positive and vice versa. This is not the truth the switching of polarities it is a reference from going from the dark ages where the earth is ruled by the demi urge, the male energy to being ruled by the female energy {Sophia} as the Gnostics call our creator. The creator as a whole is 95 percent female and 5 percent male, we are all male and female that's why we can say father in heaven and its correct, yet when this is said, we are talking to the male aspect of the creator. We can easily see in the past times when the earth has been in a female polarity, the men wearing wigs to look like the woman, darkness cannot stop the polarity change, but they can easily over polarize it which is exactly what they do. They force the polarity to the extreme pole, so it causes an unbalance. We are currently seeing this with darkworker women only healing and retreats etc. This separation will cause a rift between the male and female. This rift the darkness will use to control, polarity is how the masses are steered. Everyone is polarized to something! We need to heal as a group, a tribe. We need to heal as man and woman and come together as a single unit. This would additionally heal the generational karma as well as unite the male and female.

KARMA

Is the first topic I would like to discuss regarding ascension. Many beings here try to program their selves that karma does not exist, this makes me chuckle, if only! Yes, mentalism is the highest principal but there are laws that govern these things set forth by the most high, your thoughts cannot over power the creators laws. Earth a school to teach us, it is that karma that is the master teacher. Karma is very simple; you shall reap what you sow! clearly written in the bible. The Christian church taken over long ago by the Freemasons; The Society of Jesus run by the Jesuits, their Freemason preachers only preach the Abrahamic doctrine. The Abrahamic movement is the dark one's religion, these beings secretly worship their freemason god Jahbulon, the Rasta JAH! Another reference to this hidden god, no you cannot sacrifice animals or humans? Why do people not judge this more accurately? Remember Pagan means citizen, what was pagan means of the common people!

To enter heaven on earth, the garden of Eden you cannot have any karma from past lives or this current life! This alone is highly hilarious to me because at the present time all the dark workers are trying to get past life regressions to release their past life karma. They think this will allow them to make the ascension, sadly this is not even close to being true. These dark workers have no idea of the requirements. When we do a past life regression if the client is carrying past life karma {I say carrying because it's an energetic weight the person carries, it literally will hold you down into the lower vibrations} The client will cry when they look at the situation that caused the karma. Then and only then will this life's karma start to come into balance. In my first past life regression I was carrying past life karma and I looked at the situation which caused it and I cried like a baby for a good ten minutes, but it did not stop there, omg I wish. I had led a sinners life thinking no one was watching or judging what

I did, I had lied and cheated and hurt people! This karma started coming back to bring my balance back to even. Let me explain further, think of karma as a sliding scale! When we are judged at death, we will be made to feel all the good and the bad we put out into the world. If we have not put out more love and joy more hate than grief, we fail that life and it must be re lived, this is where past life karma comes in! if the balance is close, we are allowed to bring karma forward into the next life. It is like starting the life with a debt. My personal life was chosen to start with this energetic debt, this chosen to hide my energy, to hide my light and vibration. All laws that govern the earth construct are bendable, not breakable but we can manipulate them in accordance with the hermetic principals. What I speak of is called the scepter of power in magic. Thoth being the being that's present at each soul's judgement, the heart against a feather. This energetic lightness is what the QHHT people are claiming as their healing, all past life clients will feel lighter after their session. QHHT does not heal or cure illness or disease. When I investigated their claims after learning this modality and finding it did not heal anything, I was shocked to find that the only reference to any actual healing was Dolores claiming she saw the healings, I could not find any testimonials in video. Anyone can write a written testimonial; this is why I get my clients to make a video of their results. The others can watch and see the sessions as well as the clients' words about their experience. Having a karma free life alone will not get you into the garden of Eden! But it is the biggest obstacle. When you see a person that crippled or missing body parts this is karma, they have physically hurt others in past lives.

Note

These dark masters use a soul possession to skip karma and stay on the earth plane and not go through the reincarnation cycle or they would all be effed up so bad, all lame and crippled if not totally destroyed karma from their actions. They use free will at their secret lodges to possess another human's body to be able to live in this world.

Next topic I would like to discuss is entity attachments and how these will play into the ascension. My research here started with the mini-ice age of the

1750s there are massive clues hidden here. These ascensions happen at different times for each human generates their own reality they experience; these timelines are constantly adjusted by the angels and the divine to give many opportunities to ascend and to do the inner work. These ascension's happening at different times is one reason we are locked down from travel, so others cannot see what is going on. The mini mace age of the 1750s was the last major ascension and reset. Best I can tell it spanned about 100 years start to finish. The Black death! The plaque! What is it? Why did it come then mysteriously disappear? Great questions that today we have the answers too. These black spots that emerged on people are not caused by a rat or a bacterium, no no! these are caused by entity attachments. I have found this already starting again. An entity attachment is a vibration of death anger etc., these are very low vibrations that are attached to humans. In a AQHT session the color of the entity attachment shows its vibration, red anger yellow sorrow and black is the lowest. As the vibration is raising on earth and through the collective things that do not match the vibrations become necrotic. Example if I have a nasty attachment attached to my ankle and the vibration gets really high it will cause the area to turn black and for the tissues to die! My research has already proven all infections are caused by entity attachments. I have personally experienced this myself, after a conjuring attack from some Freemasons my ankle started turning black and swelling, I immediately did a AQHT session, and it immediately went away. Everything happens for a reason and these reasons are always dual in nature, matter a fact nothing can be created here unless it serves both light and dark. This situation taught me that the black death is caused by these entity attachments and can easily be cured. This ascension being the biggest ever that humanity will ever experience it was paramount that we have this knowledge, The black death we will see this time will be 10k times worse than the 1750s. The only way to heal and prevent this is with the AQHT modality and doing it on a regular basis. Receiving a AQHT session every month to three months as needed dependent on what the client has experienced since their last session will take away the need for 90 percent of all the current need for medical treatment. The hospitals are failing as we speak, my business is booming because the people have lost trust in the health care system and presently, they will enforce the mark of the beast and in turn refuse to treat anyone that's didn't get jabbed. Think about it like this, it is my charge to keep these lower vibrations out of the garden of Eden, first off, they can and are used in bad magic {conjuring aka Freemason and Druid magic} in the 7D energy we don't really get sick much as these nasty attachments are not present there. They will not be allowed, if you have nasty attachments, you will most likely experience the Black Death before the rapture happens.

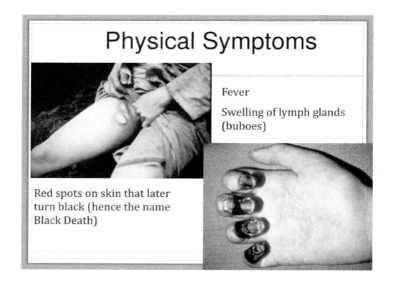

Physical Symptoms

Fever

Swelling of lymph glands (buboes)

Red spots on skin that later turn black (hence the name Black Death)

These are caused by entity attachments, I have already seen this in my clients and cured it successfully by removing the attachments.

LOVE

This is the one that will keep all darkworkers out of Eden. We must have love for all beings, the heart itself will be weighed. This cannot be faked or bypassed. Many darkworkers are privy to what is going on and have come to me to get healed, Freemasons revoking their oaths like rats off a sinking ship! I heal all as long as they do not attack me or mess with my energies. These beings after their sessions are vibrationally lighter but they lacked empathy and love and compassion for ALL beings here. These beings some have even stopped eating meat. Let me take some time to discuss this. Draconian's have developed a jibby jab that is allowing them to live in these higher vibrations and not eat meat. The talk of the boosters is in reference to this. There are different concoctions in these jabs. The one for humans is meant to modify their dna. This has several objectives. Remember everything created here has dual purposes. The jabs for humans are sterilizing them so they cannot reproduce {the same exact way the Draco's enslaved the Grays, they took away their ability to reproduce in the physical} additionally when healing these clients I found that their eyes had turned all black, I have a spiritual gift {the all seeing eye of Horus} I see peoples souls and the colors I see tells me who and what they are and how far on their journey to enlightenment as well as how conscious they are. All souls start out with black eyes, that's why most have a dark circle around the outside, when fully conscious and karma free there will be no dark circle around the eye and their eyes become very light in color, many actually change color. It's very normal for a vegans eyes to become lighter. This shows us the vibration of their soul. This sterilization is why there are thousands of pregnant women that got jabbed and lost their babies. When doing sessions on these clients it was found that ALL their chakras had been shut down. Effectively disconnecting them from source.

Authors note

Its blows my mind that all the missing people is not being noticed by the masses. People have ascended out of the slave matrix, they are not retired or collecting unemployment, they have started ascending towards the Garden. To make this obvious I have worked my ass off giving sessions to any that would take them at first, this done to raise the collective's vibration. Now I am commanded to not give sessions unless they are on the right path, non-meat eaters and learning magic and love in their hearts. I had to make it apparent. Yet the masses still don't see it, soon this will change, all the healers doing their work has ascended so many that the system is in full collapse as we speak.

Love is so misunderstood, let's go over some examples. We are taught to heal ourselves first, we are taught to love ourselves first,{self-love is the hardest lesson to learn} after we accomplish this then we are to apply these principals to the collective, the micro to the macro. If I have learned to love myself, then I have to learn love for all beings. An example is this, Love for all living beings will have me not eat or support anything that enslaves or kills animals. We are all one! This means humans incarnate as animals first, except dogs, these are ascended masters coming to support the humans, your world is backwards, dog is God backwards yes? If I learn to heal myself then I must share this with the world to help others heal too. If I have love for all beings and someone tries to lock up others or force them into bad decisions, then it is my job to speak up and stand up for the highest good of all beings. Never be silent when lies are spoken. Creator gave man dominion over earth, this means it is our job {the Christian turn the other cheek and God moves in mysterious ways, let God handle it doctrine has really brainwashed the people} Jesus revolted against the TAX man, Taxation is theft! the current US citizen is taxed at approximately 60 percent of all their earnings. Love for all beings will have the citizen stop working in the system and supporting it by paying taxes, yes, they can take money, but there is no law requiring a human to file a tax return. It is all free will; darkness uses fear to manipulate the peoples free will. Dark workers fail in the love area so bad they will never ascend by trying to rid their life of the karma and not eating meat, it simply will not cut it. This day of judgement that is coming is a vibrational weight, either make it or not, this also applies to me as well.

Note

The planet of love is Venus! The morning star! Its easily visible in the morning sun rise. Arc Angel Lucifer {a female angel} demonized by the Christians, as well as Friday, {Freya's day} also the day of Venus and especially Friday the 13th, 13 being the highest manifesting number we have. This angel is the angel that brings enlightenment to those elect adapts that have attained the knowledge and vibration of love.

Remember everything u were taught is backwards, these beings condemn anything that is love and female.

Love is so multifaceted, the turn the other cheek doctrine is not of love, the don't judge doctrine is not of love. You chose to come here to be judged and to judge others. Obviously, we don't judge people for ignorant stuff like skin color, who they chose to partner with, etc. we judge people for eating the flesh of the creators' beings, for swindling others into taking a jibby jab, we judge others for their silence, silence is compliance, and no choice is a choice. Our mandate is to live in unison with all beings as much as possible that we can. Let's look at some examples, if you pay a home payment, you are supporting the enslavement of others. No one owns this land here it's all ours to use and share and to take care of. They day they convinced humans that land can be owned is the day they made the human population homeless, all must pay to exist. If you make a car payment you are supporting that money debt system that has caused this coming crash! The economic collapse is our fault. A credit system is a system of enslavement. If you pay your power bill you are supporting the stealing of energy for profit adding to the human enslavement. If you work a job that supports any of these things you are supporting that matrix, it is very simple withdraw your energy and it will die all on its own, no fighting no wars, focus and work towards a free peaceful life for all beings. Moving forward we are moving out of the duality energy and into the oneness energy, those that are creating for the highest good of all beings are the ones that will be rewarded and abundant. You should be off grid and self-sustainable power food water and healing. Then you will be greatly rewarded and on your way ascending to Eden. We are going home to the Garden. The Meek shall inherit the earth.

These are the main things that will keep you from ascending, lets discuss how the ascension experience actually works. At special times on earth the Ascension window is open, for souls that are ready to experience heaven on earth. Christians are told they must die to experience heaven; this is true for most of them as they are the army of darkness used to harvest their energy for the dark master. They eat flesh and this alone will block them entry, the Christians in general just do not carry the vibration to access this in their physical life, an example here is when they pray, they say amen after their prayers this is for the god Amun, also known as Mercury the closest planet to the sun. They use this god to carry their prayers to the creator because they do not carry the vibration to access the creator directly. Some will wake up and see the lies in their cult religion, but most do not. These times are easy to spot when we look at history, they will always be accompanied by the whole virus and the forcing of mask wearing agenda. The last three that really stick out is the 400-year reset. A reset ascension is different than a mini ascension as I call them. The 400-year reset ascension is nearly the same as the ascension we are going through now. The big difference is that this ascension is additionally an end of a cycle ascension. The Creator has tricked the darkness, let me explain, in past ascensions there has always been two timelines after separation, separation has already occurred presently and instead of there being a separation of a higher and a lower world {darkness counts on going with the lower vibrational world to easily take over. This time the divine is destroying these lower timelines as we go. Either ascend or die! It's very simple we are all in this together} These ends of cycle ascension is very much more destructive and earth changing. The biggest difference in this reset and all the other resets is that this ascension is the evolution of humanity. Humans are returning to the garden of Eden {aka heaven on earth} Humanity was violently ripped out of the garden of Eden vibration by some 5th dimensional beings that decided to take over humanity!

This is the flood story in the bible, which was stolen from the epic of Gilgamesh, and then they manipulated the words to make people believe that the word god means the creator of all and that the great deluge was from the divine, it was not! The Draconian's drilled through the firmament in Antarctica, anyone know of any groups in Antarctica? The one place on earth you are not allowed to go. We have remote viewed them there and yes, they are desperately trying to drill through the firmament again. It's all about vibration, the garden of Eden is 7D, the slave matrix is 3D, The Draconian's came from another dimension {5D} and yes, another construct not planet. These beings were created to manipulate energies in service of creation. The many stories of the Nehalem and the Anunnaki coming down {from a higher vibration, not space} is all true. These beings took over the present earth construct we live in so they could be worshipped like the creator gods, the Elohim, these are humans. These Draconian's are not gods, yet to a physical human they might appear so, they are vibrational masters, they easily see and control vibrations, easily read your mind and manipulate your thoughts dreams and vibration {Draconian's must eat dead flesh to stay in this vibration, they have a hunger for flesh like no other, it weighs them down, when they do not eat flesh, they get really sick and die} These beings can easily control humans' minds and dreams, the dream state is their strongest weapon. People think if they have a dream, it only from their higher self, this just is not true and is opposite of truth. Draconian's are very much physically stronger than the humans, especially after thousands of years of genetic manipulation degrading the physical humans' bodies. This is why we could not beat them in a physical fight. Therefore, they colonized the entire earth. Fortunately, we knew all this 100k years ago and set plans in motion that would put the final battle for humanities freedom into a venue that would be advantageous to the humans. Draconian are a base 12 being, this won't make much sense to you as this is alien quantum mechanics, but I'll try to explain. The humans here in this present incarnation are a base 10 being {one means creation in Hermetics} the human a creator being, this means that their thoughts and feelings actually create the reality we experience.

Thus, why the Draco's use their tell a lie vision to control humanities minds and thus controlling their manifestations. A human can never turn off their manifesting, it runs 24 hours a day. The only way to change this is to re program their minds and turn off the tv. Have you noticed? every news station looks like it is loaded with gold inside? they have elaborate security and fences, barber wire etc. Why the need for all this massive security? These brainwashing stations were paramount to take out, the divine took care of this. A base 10 being is a creator, a base 12 an energy manipulator {1 means creation 2 means choice add it up to 3, 3 is the conscious mind and is also male, 3 overall means energy for change} The kicker here is a fully ascended god is a base 13 being {1 means creation 3 energy for change, add it up to 4 which means earth}. This is a human that has incarnated in the earth construct and graduated. Humans can absolutely become living gods. That's why they are here, to seek enlightenment and to unlock and learn how to control their creation abilities. A base 13 being has reached the eternal level, to be eternal means you become a living consciousness that lives jumping life to life as so desired in league with the creator's divine plan. This cycle reached the end of the present cycle in 2012, this means all the beings that don't make it get recycled to source. These very nefarious beings seek to be like the most high, to be a creator and to be worshipped like the gods. Fortunately for us their arrogance shows us exactly who and what they are. In the present energy we can all see them with our physical eyes. I get so excited when I see them out in the stores wearing their masks to hide their very sharp teeth {easiest to spot, look on the top they will have a vampire tooth and behind them they will all be very sharp} and their dark sunglasses. These are a sure-fire way to see them in person.

NOTE

We are dealing with a very capable being, they can easily read our thoughts and easily manipulate our vibrations, empathy alone cannot be trusted one must use discernment in conjunction with all our gifts. Example: a person presents as a healer yet eats fish, is this person of the light? Can you trust them? This answer is a no, an empath cannot eat dead flesh, they feel the karma, a

healer would never eat the creators' beings after awakening to the fact that we are all one, this includes all animals. All dreams must be scrutinized to find out if it was from an outside source or our own higher self.

These base12 Draco's are scared to death at this point, there has never been so much light on the earth, second the son of man walks among us, this base 13 creator being watches over humanity and guides our evolution. No being here can stop this being! The time of the prophecies are now. This being known falsely as Jesus is the oldest incarnated being in this solar system.

The next ascension event I want to examine is the Carrington event of 1859. Signs of the upcoming Solar flash started on August 28th when smaller CME {coronal mass ejection} starting to interrupt the electrical grids and communications, it lasted through sept 2nd, so we are told. These events are currently happening again right now as we speak, we are receiving elevated solar storms, which just caused an underground eruption near Tonga and Tsunamis all around the pacific ring of fire. The divine will turn off the Draco's brainwashing system. I was instructed to not worry about this that THEY would handle it. This event also creates the norther lights to be seen as far as the tropics as we are also seeing today. The next event was in the Spanish flu of 1918. This timeline reeks of ascension. In times that the vibration starts to raise the Draco's combat it with massive fear, war and poverty. First, we have the first world war starting for America in 1917, then the Spanish flu in 1918, then the stock market crash of 1929 which put the world and America into poverty. These beings use gold as money and do not consider fiat money to be real money, they constantly do this boom bust cycle to take away the wealth from the people. All these signs tell me that there was some kind of ascension going on! This shows the Draco's were trying to bring down the vibration of the collective! We also have Edgar Cayce present on earth healing people like Jesus. Edgar Cayce died in 1945, This is where Dolores Cannon stole her QHHT technique from. She a Draco reptilian herself did not create it.

Let's go over some general things regarding ascension, no we do not ascend all the way back to a being of pure light. This always makes me laugh, what would be the purpose of incarnating into a physical body? To just return to our true form light. Kind of redundant if you ask me. How high we ascend is individual, anything under 7D does not make it and is the end of days {tribulation} timelines. Next up its all individual, if you do not carry the vibration you do not get access to 7D {if you cannot control your thoughts and banish negative ones, you do not get unlimited creation abilities, to give these people access to their full powers and not be able to control their thoughts would be like handing a 5 year old a loaded gun} you must have a basic understanding of magic and manifestation and control our mental abilities to ascend. No one with karma ascends, past or present life {eating meat creates karma and keeps a person from ascending} We have to seek and learn to live outside the system with no money, to live in unison with all beings. This being said: there will be beings that are lacking in some areas but carry a high degree of love in their hearts, like ethical Vegans. These beings clearly understand the importance of thall shall not kill! Vegans are Jesus' people, not the Christians. When we look back at our very convoluted history, we see orphan trains as well as mass numbers of children with missing parents. These parents didn't throw away their kids, these kids are left over from an ascension. The parents born long before their kids {is a kid a baby goat? Do the Draco's worship the Baphomet, Jahbulon? the goat god?} these beings born into an older, darker energy have more work to do to upgrade their bodies and their soul, the kids are born into a lighter energy. Almost all the kids ascend, so this is why we see thousands of kids with no parents, America, England, Australia. All clearly documented and easy to research.

When I would do future life regressions the clients often saw 20 to 30 kids a piece that each tribe were raising, these kids ascended, and their parents did not. This is actually much more complicated than just this and a person's energy or KA as we called it in Atlantean times, the Ka is split and a version of that person's self actually goes both ways so that the beings that didn't ascend do not really know. When asked about in the regressions we were told many do know something is different after the ascension. Many are being programmed that an event a solar flash will appear, and they will know, this too is not true and true, as each human generates their own reality, I found some would experience 10 days of darkness, an eruption blocking out the sun? Yellowstone will erupt soon covering half the world with ash, or a solar flash? these are already happening. I found some people would not know any difference. They would go to sleep one day and the next day the world was just different. It all depends on the persons programming and their soul contracts on what they chose to experience. The darkness always wants you to look outside of yourself, a collective event! Aliens are outside you! God is outside you! Someone will come save you! The power of the magician's sleight of hand is clearly a powerful tool indeed! What is the ultimate deception the darkness is hiding from you? The grand solar minimum, the mini-ice age that comes roughly every 400 years. The Earth is the ultimate reset tool. Humans are but a flea on a dog's back in relation to Gaia. It is not you, it's not CO_2, it's the sun that is the ultimate master of our destiny and what happens on earth. There are two worlds that have existed here up to this point in time, as we move into the ascending age and the oneness energy the bottom world gets closed out completely! This is the way planets evolve. The Divine knowing the forever time just waited, minimizing the colonization of the planet by darkness so that it did not destroy humanity or Gaia. Darkness wants us to get mad and fight, this is their food, war on drugs, fight cancer etc. these beings from another dimension desperately need these dark energies to survive {Jesus said love thy enemy} If we send them love for the lessons rather than anger and hatred, we take away their power and they starve.

Let us discuss the obstacles the darkness has created to keep you from ascending. Freemasons have Masonic tracing boards to show the obstacles they created to keep you from ascending. First obstacle is shown by the symbol of the Christian cross. Hermetics are explained through symbolism colors and numbers. Let us Hermetically examine the Christian cross. The first thing that stands out is that its longer on the bottom than the top, this means its polarized to the physical world {the opposite of spirituality is materialism} Naholo a lover of things! The next thing is its shown as a wooden cross {in magic wood is used when binding things, these people by their oath, do you accept Jesus Christ as your lord and savior? Free will and an oath here} Jesus is usually shown bound down to that wooden cross, this is a huge magical binding and deception. The Ankh has a circle on top,

why the major difference? When we learn the occulted {means hidden} Mystery religion of Atlantis
{Hermetics} you gain eternal life and are able to re-
incarnate at will and to live eternally jumping body
to body through time. The Christian cross is a straight line on the top, this is showing you that these
beings will only live once and then be recycled back
to source. The modern Christian church is the army
of darkness the dark one created for the final battle.
One wanting to ascend will have to wake up to the
programming that we in the west are raised with,
to see it as a cult deep with secret magical rituals to
harvest energy. The word god means to invoke, not
the creator of ALL.

The next obstacle on the masonic tracing board is
the anchor, this is very widespread in its meanings.
Anything that anchors you to keep you from moving, some examples are your debt payments, your
house mortgage, your materiel stuff. It was the most
liberating thing to give away and sell all my stuff and
become a minimalist, it was like I shed a thousand
pounds in a day. Another anchor that's directly tied
to the Christian brainwashing is family, Christians
are taught the family u incarnated into you must ho-

nor them and be obedient unto them. This is so not true, let me explain if your father is toxic, you need and have to cut them out of your life. It matters not if you are related unto them, unfortunately these are the most toxic of situations when dealing with toxic family members. A lot of Christian churches display the anchor as well {a soul's harbor} if a ship is in harbor it is not moving on its journey now is it?

The next symbol they use is the symbol of a heart, first off, the heart shape is actually two hearts connected to make this shape as an actual human heart only makes half the shape. The very last obstacle we have to overcome and to raise our vibration too is love {there is a war against love} First we must learn self-love {hardest lesson I ever leaned, this lesson is never over} next we must learn love for all beings, plants, insects, animals, Gaia, other humans and most of all the darkness. If you eat animals, you do not have love for all beings now do you?

The biggest hidden secret in the heart symbol is we must come into union with our divine partnership, it is this union that creates massive amounts of love and gratitude. The dark workers on the social medias are telling people you don't need your person just focus on you, you complete yourself and do not need to seek them. Sadly, this is true and not true, yes, we must do the inner work to heal and be happy, so we are able to show up and be present for our divine union. {while on this topic I'd like to share what the creator told me, she said we only get one so pick carefully! These people spreading the open and polyamorous relationships are not going to ascend} The very last step is to unite with our person and become one, a single unit moving together in unison creating the life that both beings seek.

THE TWIN FLAME
DECEPTION

This is a huge deception being carried out by darkness! Maybe the biggest ever. First let's explain what a twin flame is and the different types of unions we encounter. First, the most common, these are given in the order of most common to the rarest. The Karmic partner! this is because each one we have a soul contract with to teach us something and most of us have many karmic partners on our journey. {again the Christians condemned divorce, a way to stop people from finding their true love} Next up is the Divine Union! These are our chosen partners and where the darkness is selling these as twin flame unions. These unions will have many synchronicities, they feel like the entire universe is telling you to go this direction {sadly Draconian's and

Reptilians as well as insectoids can manipulate our energy to provide us false synchronicities} Love is the battlefield! The rarest of all is the Twin Flame! These souls only come together in their last incarnation ever, after their union they will evolve back into one being and become another sun somewhere in the multiverse. These are really easy to spot. The twin flame union will be both healers. The healer is the closet a being can be to source on its journey back to source. Well, that takes out 99 percent of all the so-called twin flames. Next up is the eyes, the eyes are the window to the soul! If the TWINS eyes are not exactly the same it's not the same soul, one cannot have blue eyes and the other brown. These twins are pushed by darkness to keep people from moving onto their karmic partnerships they need to grow, I see it all the time a client tells me I'm a twin, but the other person doesn't know it and they are married but I am waiting for them! Sadly, no this is not their twin and them waiting is them not moving on and learning their chosen lessons. Twins make up .01 percent of the population so there could not be thousands of them as these people are pretending. On our souljurn back to light, the closer we get back to source the more we will emulate the lights characteristics. Example the light heals all, we the incarnated being will be a working healer, anyone that not a healer is not close to the love! Additionally, source could care less about your money or stuff! A being that enlightened will have sworn off money and materiel stuff. We see many dark workers trying to speak enlightenment, yet they have no knowledge of it except the general stuff, we are all one, we are all light, we are all love etc. The darkness manipulating people's empathy and thoughts they are able to block many divine unions. The divine union is the one we should all be seeking not the I'm a twin flame deception.

To ascend you must step out of your comfort zone and do a trust fall with spirit. You must walk a path similar to Jesus' parables. You must conquer fear, you must give up all materiel attachment. {how powerful is a person that cannot be controlled by fear or by materiel things?} we must climb the ladder and up the vibrational realities until we are knocking on Eden's door. This vibrational realm is very guarded. Only those that have a pure heart and have done the inner work will be granted entry. The hidden secret is that we all can ascend to the garden of Eden and experience heaven on earth in this life. This whole construct was created for us to be at this magical vibration where we create in real time as a God or Goddess should. To focus on the darkness and what they did to put humanity into this situation is not useful at this level. Its paramount to understand how we got here, but all must be forgiven and healed. To fight anything means we are creating a negative energy that these dark beings seek and need, we will fight nothing, we will stand in unity and loving defiance to the oppression and colonization of planet earth.

The only way to survive is to Ascend!

In Conclusion I want to say thank you to the Creator! Gaia! And all my many supporters light and dark I send you love for the lessons. There is no good or bad, just lessons we learn, learn them and move on keep climbing! You got this!

I look into the eyes of the beings that I meet and what I see blows my mind, it is such a huge deception of the reality that I thought I lived in compared to the real reality that exists. 5700 years ago, a darkness descended into this realm, in this cycle the Anunnaki or Nephilim or fallen angels descended into this realm and started taking it over again. This cycle repeats during the descending age, and once the earth starts into the ascending age this cycle is closed out and will not return for another 12k years, never again will the window for this darkness to come back in be open. these beings just cannot match the vibration of love, remember they eat meat to weigh themselves down to stay in this vibration.

I see a world that is going to freak out so many people as their spiritual eyesight is opened, and all humans sight will open during this time. {except the jibby jabbed} I see a race of aliens that are ruling over the human race, I see a group of beings that eat humans. When this knowledge hits the mainstream, all hell will break out overnight. The preferred food for the draconian's is human meat, young girls ages 5 to 10. The freemasons have cars set up to move these kidnapped kids, they will have completely blacked out windows and usually a large freemason sticker to let the other aliens know that this is a transport car and to not stop it. Draconian's have killed, lied, raped and stolen everything from the humans. As I look into the eyes of the Draconian's I come into contact with I see and feel their massive fear, they know they are trapped and that they all will have to answer for their actions.

Draconian's and every other being that has consciousness came from source, Source is mother, mother has a bunch of kids that will not get along! How to fix this issue? She decided to lock us all in until we get along. The message is super simple, either get along and work together or perish! Its that simple. The sooner we work together the more of our people will survive. I was told early on that very few draconian's or freemasons will survive. They just will not turn to love.

My heart is heavy as I know soon the war between the Draco's and the humans will erupt into the mainstream soon.

It was my call which way to go here, {remember the realm is greatly affected by the beings that are incarnated} I saw the Draco's timeline where they tricked humans into fighting each other yet again, I asked can we stop the fighting and killing? Creator said no. I decided then if life must be lost and wars fought then let the humans fight for their survival and their freedom. If there was to be loss of the physical life, then it would be best served fighting for real freedom!

Careful which side you pick! One choice leads to an eternal soul death and the other choice well that leads to eternal life and to experience the garden of Eden for the first time on earth since the fall of Atlantis some approximately 50k years ago.

Pick wisely and much Love friend.

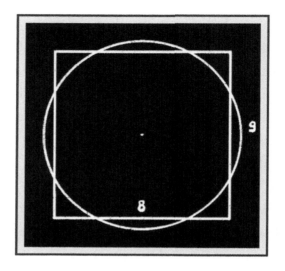

The square represents the man, and the
circle represents the Woman.

To Heal and ascend find me
@ clintonwithrowqhht.com

To follow me on a free speech platform subscribe @
https://odysee.com/@CosmicQuantumAwakening:3

Printed in Great Britain
by Amazon

36292526R00098